The Blanket of Blessings

Betty L. Milne

PublishAmerica
Baltimore

© 2011 by Betty L. Milne.
All rights reserved. No part of this book may be reproduced, stored in a retrieval system or transmitted in any form or by any means without the prior written permission of the publishers, except by a reviewer who may quote brief passages in a review to be printed in a newspaper, magazine or journal.

First printing

All characters in this book are fictitious, and any resemblance to real persons, living or dead, is coincidental.

PublishAmerica has allowed this work to remain exactly as the author intended, verbatim, without editorial input.

Photo used in cover design provided by Gail Augustine

Softcover 9781462653508
PUBLISHED BY PUBLISHAMERICA, LLLP
www.publishamerica.com
Baltimore

Printed in the United States of America

~ This book is lovingly dedicated to my wonderful mother, Roberta L. Tuvey, who generously blanketed me with blessings and stitched each one into my heart. ~

CONTENTS

CHAPTER ONE..................................7
CHAPTER TWO.................................21
CHAPTER THREE..............................59
CHAPTER FOUR................................78
CHAPTER FIVE.................................89
CHAPTER SIX..................................107
CHAPTER SEVEN.............................122
CHAPTER EIGHT..............................134
CHAPTER NINE................................146
CHAPTER TEN.................................163
CHAPTER ELEVEN...........................173
CHAPTER TWELVE..........................190
CHAPTER THIRTEEN.......................198
CHAPTER FOURTEEN.....................207
CHAPTER FIFTEEN..........................218
CHAPTER SIXTEEN.........................225
CHAPTER SEVENTEEN...................232
CHAPTER EIGHTEEN......................242
CHAPTER NINETEEN......................251

CHAPTER ONE

The County Fair

The wonderful aromas from the kitchen wafted through the rest of the small farm house. Fresh baked apple and peach pies sat on the kitchen table, cooling from the hot oven. Angie admired her mother, Faith, as much as a 10 year old girl could. After all, her mother made the best pies in Boone County and always won the Best of Show Blue Ribbons. Well, nearly always. Once in a great while, Edith Hopkins would give her mother a run for the ribbon and Edith's cherry pie would claim the prize. This only encouraged the anticipation for the upcoming fair and that day had finally arrived. The 1853 Boone County Fair began this very day, a time to mark the end of summer filled with fresh produce, baked goods, handmade crafts, farm animals, and friendly competition among friends and strangers alike. This day always brought excitement to the Owens household. But there was one entry that Faith was sure to win every year. Angie's mother made the most beautiful crocheted blankets anyone had ever seen.

Angie wandered into the tidy little living room and ran her slender fingers over the delicately knotted yarn and dreamed of winning a blue ribbon of her own.

"Come children," her mother called as she emerged from the kitchen holding a pie carefully sandwiched between two kitchen towels. "We need to get these pies and my blanket to the fair. We can't be late."

Her little brother came running clumsily down the stairs. Angie knew that one day he would trip and fall headlong if he continued his random stair jumping. "Be careful, Billy," Angie warned, "You'll fall and hurt yourself!"

"He's alright," her mother smiled, "He's just excited."

"I know, but…" Angie protested.

"Hush now, dear" Faith interrupted, "We need to get on our way. Collect the blanket and help me put everything in the wagon."

Angie gave her brother a disapproving glance and then picked up the beautiful blue-and-white afghan and held it tight to her chest. *Someday,* she thought, *I'll take* **my** *beautiful blanket to the fair."*

The old dirt roads were heavy with people carrying their entries. Most people were arriving in horse-drawn wagons, but a number of them walked from their nearby homes. Columbia, Missouri was a growing town and had the proud distinction of having the largest fair in all of the state. As the Owens wagon rambled down the center of town, Faith saw Edith Hopkins walking down the street proudly holding her cherry pie up higher than need be. Faith nodded and gave her an approving smile. She liked Edith, a contrary woman, but with a good heart and a helping hand when needed.

Angie sat forward and strained to see the entrance to the fairgrounds. Her daddy, William, was going to meet them there. He had been working in the General Store all morning, but the kind owner, George McKenna, encouraged William to take the rest of the day off. "I'm closing the store, George. No use in staying open when everyone's going to be at the fair."

George and his wife, Elma, were like family to the Owens. They ate many a meal together and told many a wild tale by the fireplace to the children's delight. Billy would always add his imagination to the stories, as 6-year-olds tend to do, making everyone laugh with the absurdness of it all. The Mckennas had no children of their own and were getting on in years, so Angie and Billy held a special place in their hearts. They'd watched these little babies grow into fine youngsters and lavished love and attention unsparingly on them.

"Someday, William," George was always pleased to say, "my General Store will be yours. I'll be too old to keep that place running, and you'll have to take over and then hand it down to Billy. Gotta keep the business in the family!" And he'd pat William on the back and smile proudly.

"You'll never be too old," William would assure him.

"There's daddy!" Angie yelled as she spotted her father standing next to George. Faith found a place under a tree to tie the horse to and waved to William and George as they approached the wagon. The children jumped down from the wagon and ran to their daddy. William scooped up Angie and said "There's my Honey Bee!"

"And just as sweet" Angie reminded him of the game they would always play. William set her back down and then held Billy up high in the air, "And how are you Snuggle Bug?"

"As snug as a bug in a rug!" Billy would always answer. William laughed and set Billy down next to Angie and then helped Faith carry her pies. Angie carried the crocheted blanket proudly in her arms, knowing that all the ladies were trying to catch a glimpse of it as she walked by.

As they arrived at the display tables, Angie asked if she could go see the prize bulls that were being shown this year. Boone County was challenging nearby Monroe County to a contest of who had the biggest beef bulls, and it had become the big attraction of the fair this year.

"Yes," Faith answered, "Take Billy with you. Keep an eye on him. Don't let him get lost."

"I won't" Angie said as she grabbed Billy's hand and ran down to the animal pens. They darted among the other sightseers nearly running into several unsuspecting people.

"Slow down!" Billy yelled, "I can't run that fast!"

"There they are!' Angie pointed toward the crowd that had gathered. "Come on, we're almost there!"

Making their way up to the front of the spectators, their eyes grew big and their mouths gaped as they gazed at the huge bulls that had been entered for competition. "I've never seen such big cows!" Angie remarked.

"Me neither!" Billy added.

After examining all six of the bulls that had been entered, the three best from each county, Angie pointed at one of the bulls from Boone County. "That's the one that's going to win! I bet that one is the biggest of all of them!"

Billy nodded his head in agreement.

"I wish we had one of those big cows. Everyone would come to visit us just so they could see the huge bull we owned and they'd think we were rich," Angie smiled.

"Yeah, they'd think we were the richest people in the whole world!" Billy agreed.

After a few minutes of dreaming, Angie pulled Billy away from the crowd and they began to walk back toward the displays. Suddenly, Angie stopped dead in her tracks.

There she was, Pearl Hubbard, the thorn in Angie's side ever since the Hubbard family moved to their town several years ago. Angie wasn't sure why she and Pearl never got along. She assumed it was because her mother always won ribbons at the fair each year and Pearl's mother never won any; at least, none that she ever saw. All Angie knew was they had ill feelings toward each other from the very beginning.

Pearl walked up to Angie, with her best friend, Betsy, at her side. Betsy was Angie's best friend before Pearl came to town, and now Betsy seemed to enjoy needling Angie every bit as much as Pearl did.

"I used to go to Angie's house," Betsy told Pearl as they both looked at Angie. "It's a very small house, you know, and only sits on a very small piece of land. Only enough for a few vegetables and a fruit tree or two. Hardly anything one could be proud of."

"It used to be just fine for you before Pearl came to town," Angie retorted.

"I was just being nice to you," Betsy said, "I felt sorry for you."

"Yes, we ALL feel sorry for you," Pearl added to the sarcasm.

"Don't feel sorry for me. After all, I'm not a little spoiled brat like you!" Angie turned to Pearl in spite.

"That's so true. I may be spoiled, but that's because you have nothing compared to me. My mother and father are rich and yours are so poor. Too bad for you!" Pearl smiled contentedly and turned her back to Angie, walking away with Betsy at her side, both laughing to each other.

I don't care, Angie told herself, *I'd rather be poor and have what I have. I have everything I need, and a better family than she'll ever have!"*

"I don't like her." Billy looked up at his sister. "She's so mean to you. And I don't like Betsy anymore either. I was gonna marry her when I grew up, but not anymore!"

"You'll find someone nicer than Betsy," Angie assured her brother. "There'll be lots of nice girls to marry when you grow up.

"Are you going to get married when you grow up?" Billy asked Angie innocently.

"No, I don't think so," Angie answered sadly, "I don't want to marry anyone but daddy, and he's already married to momma. Come on, let's go see if momma's blanket won a ribbon."

As they neared the display tables, Angie and Billy could see the judge placing the "Best of Show" ribbon on their mother's crocheted blanket, for the ninth year in a row.

Angie ran up to her mother and hugged her. "You did it momma! You won again!"

"Yes, dear." her mother hugged her back. "We are so blessed. We'll be able to sell it and buy more food for the winter and maybe a Christmas present or two."

Billy jumped up and down with the thought of Christmas coming this winter.

"Do you think I'll get a toy to play with?"

"You need a new coat this year, you're growing so fast," his mother said, ruffling his hair with her hand.

"A nice warm one like daddy's?" Billy asked with excitement.

"We'll see," Faith laughed.

"We need a few new hens this year," William reminded Faith, "It's time to put a couple old ones in the pot. They stopped laying eggs this summer."

"We should be able to afford that," Faith assured him and touched him on the shoulder, "God has blessed us very well this year."

"I don't know why He loves us so much," William shook his head in amazement, "I don't know what we've done to merit His favor, giving us each other and caring for us the way He has."

"I don't think it's anything that we've done, dear," Faith smiled, "I think God does just what He feels is best for us, whether it be easy or hard."

"I am so lucky to have you," William looked lovingly at his wife. "And to think you almost married John O'Reilly!"

"And you came and rescued me just in time!" Faith laughed.

"Your knight in shining armor!" William reminded her.

"Yes, my knight in shining armor," Faith mused, "I think God wanted us to be together. Do you think that long ago, God had designed us to meet?"

William nodded his head, "Yes I do. I think He made us for each other."

Faith smiled, "I think so too."

Billy tugged at his mother's skirt. "I'm hungry, mommy."

"I think we have enough for an ear of corn and a piece of chicken," his father said checking the change in his pocket. "Let's see what I have here."

Billy began jumping up and down again. "With butter on the corn?"

"Yes, with butter on the corn. Let's go find some," his father said as they began to walk toward the food cooking on the spits.

The Owens family found a place to sit down on the grass to enjoy their evening meal.

"We need some water," William said as he looked at their empty metal pitcher. "I'll go get some."

"I'll get it for you, daddy," Angie offered as she jumped to her feet. "I'll be right back."

She ran to the nearby supply of water barrels and waited in line for her turn to fill their pitcher. She filled the pitcher and then carefully carried the pitcher, taking care not to spill a drop.

"Where did you get that yellow hair?" Pearl laughed as she came up behind Angie. "You don't look like anybody in your family. You must have been pulled out of the wash bucket by mistake!"

"I look like my grandma!" Angie stuck her face in Pearl's. "And there's nothing wrong with my hair! My daddy says it looks pretty!"

"Pretty if you're a horse!" Pearl grinned and brought her nose closer to Angie's nose.

"Oh yeah? Well, your hair looks like an old brown weasel on top of your head!" Angie retorted as she threw the water from the pitcher down the front of Pearl's dress.

Pearl screamed in disgust and yelled at Angie, "You're in big trouble now! Wait until my mother sees what you've done! She'll make sure your mother spanks you for this!"

"Girls, girls!' Elma stepped in separating Angie and Pearl, "That's enough of that nonsense! Why you two act just like you're sisters!"

George stood nearby laughing to himself.

"No we don't" Angie protested, "She is NOT my sister!"

"Well, come along dear. It's time to find your family," Elma said as she took Angie by the hand and led her away. As she walked away, Angie turned and made a 'mad' face at Pearl causing Pearl to react with an even 'madder' face' and then Pearl ran to find her mother.

"But I have to get some water for daddy," Angie told Elma.

"Well, if you weren't throwing it at your friends, you'd probably have plenty of water for your father," George laughed. "Let's go over to the water barrels and wait in line."

The word soon spread that the main prize of the fair went to one of the Boone County beef bulls and would fetch a lot of money.

"I knew it!" Angie said to her family and the McKennas as they were leaving the fair. "Didn't I tell you that big bull from Boone County was going to win?" she looked to her brother for verification.

He nodded his head and yawned, growing tired with the day's excitement.

The McKennas waved goodbye and headed for their home as William untied the horses.

"There you are!" Cora yelled at the top of her lungs and came stomping over to the Owens. "I've been looking for you all evening. Look what your daughter did to my daughter!"

Pearl's mother had her squarely by the arm and shoved Pearl in front of her as if to put her on display.

"What's the matter?" William asked.

"Can't you see for yourself?!" Cora remarked. "Your daughter doused Pearl with water. Not only could she have ruined Pearl's new dress, Pearl could catch her death of cold, and for no good reason. You need to do something about that child of yours! She's a big problem for this community!"

Faith ushered the children quickly into the wagon.

William turned to Angie and asked, "Did you throw water at Pearl, Angie?"

"Yes, daddy," Angie quietly answered, but then spoke up, "but she was saying mean things to me!"

"I hardly think so!" Cora objected.

"I'm very sorry, Mrs. Hubbard, "William said earnestly. "We'll deal with Angie when we get home tonight."

"Well, I should think so!" Cora agreed. "And if you don't, then I will be forced to do so myself!"

"That won't be necessary," William said as he climbed up on the wagon and took the reins. "Have a good evening, Mrs. Hubbard."

He pulled the reins and guided the horses down the road. As the Owens were returning home from the fair, Angie fretted about being in trouble with her father.

"I'm sorry, daddy," she said loud enough for him to hear her.

"Well, sweetheart," her father began, "you probably had good reason, but that doesn't make what you did right. You can't go around trying to get back at everyone who hurts your feelings."

"I know," Angie agreed, "Are you going to punish me?"

After a bit of silence, William answered, "Well, I guess I'll have to. I want you to go out and help me in the vegetable garden tomorrow. Weeds need to be pulled and vegetables need to be gathered. No sleeping in. We'll be starting at daybreak."

She didn't relish that kind of punishment. She didn't like working in the yard, and getting her hands dirty, and William was well aware of this. But as long as she was working alongside her daddy, it would be alright.

Angie began proudly thinking about the many ribbons her mother won at the fair again this year, even taking home the Best Pie ribbon, to Edith Hopkin's displeasure. *This was the best year ever!* Angie smiled to herself. *I bet Pearl's mother didn't win anything…again!"*

Unpleasant thoughts about Pearl began to run through her mind and she had an anger building inside her.

"Momma," Angie caught her mother's attention. "Why does Pearl hate me so much?"

"I don't think she hates you dear," her mother smiled. "She might be jealous of you. Most of the time, people are mean to others because they feel inferior."

"Jealous of me? But we're poor. She has everything she wants!" Angie remarked with a confused look on her face.

"She may have everything she wants," Faith said kindly, "but she has very little of what she needs. That is where you are rich and she is poor."

Angie thought about her mother's words, trying to figure out what her mother was trying to tell her. The anger toward Pearl began to subside. She sat quietly and stroked Billy's hair as his head rested on her lap, fast asleep from his busy day at the fair.

Sometimes you're not such a bad brother," Angie smiled as she looked down at the little boy asleep on her lap. She looked up at her father and mother in the front seat. *I do have everything I need, and that does make me rich!*

****

CHAPTER TWO

The Blanket

The next morning Angie ran down the stairs to the kitchen where her mother was already fixing breakfast for the family.

"Momma, I had a dream last night, all about making my very own crocheted blanket. It had lots of colors, like a rainbow. Will you teach me how to make one? Please?" Angie begged.

Faith smiled at Angie as she turned from stirring the pot of oatmeal, a little amused by her daughter's plea. "I think you're old enough to learn how to crochet. But you'll have to earn your own yarn. We barely earn enough money to buy yarn for my yearly blanket that we sell at the fair."

"I can earn my own money, momma, I promise!" Angie exclaimed with a huge smile on her face. "I'll find a way".

"I'm sure you will," Faith smiled, "I'm very sure you will. Now you'd better grab a bite to eat and join your father out in the yard. He's waiting for you to help him in the garden."

Angie sat down to the table and ate quickly and then ran outside to join William.

"What do you want me to do, daddy?" she called as she ran up to him.

"Weed the gardens" her father answered.

"Can I pick the vegetables instead?" she asked, dreading the idea of getting her hands dirty.

"No, not right now," her father said pointing to the ground, "The weeds need pulling first."

She frowned, but obediently knelt down in the dirt and slowly pulled a couple weeds.

"Won't get it done like that," William knelt down beside her. "Get your back into it, Honey Bee. Don't be afraid of a little dirt. It won't hurt you. A little water will clean you up when you're finished."

"But it feels icky" Angie protested.

"No, it doesn't feel icky," William smiled. "It feels good. This is God's gift to us. Let this good rich dirt run through your fingers. This is what makes our vegetables grow. This soil provides us with good food and a good life."

Angie didn't quite appreciate the "good rich dirt" on her fingers the way her father did. But she determined she would work hard and get the chore over with. She realized that she wasn't going to be able to talk her way out of her punishment and decided to work as fast as she could so she could wash all this "good rich dirt" off her hands as soon as possible.

The sun grew hot and Angie grew tired. She stood up and let her tired dirty hands hang beside her. "I'm done daddy" she hollered. He looked over at her from where he was chopping wood. William set down his axe and came over to inspect Angie's completed job.

"Not bad, Honey Bee. You did a pretty good job. Alright, you can collect the vegetables now."

"But I'm tired," she protested.

"Collect the vegetables and then you're done," William instructed.

Angie didn't argue any longer. Just the idea of almost being done with her punishment was enough to give her the needed encouragement to gather what ripe vegetables she could find. She loaded the basket and took the vegetables into the house and dumped them in the sink and then went outside to fill the basket again. When she dumped the last of the vegetables in the sink, her mother thanked her and told her what a wonderful job she'd done.

"Now go wash up," Faith told her, "Dinner is almost ready. I'll need your help setting the table."

Even though Angie was tired, she knew it was part of her daily chores to set the table and help with the dishes, so she went back outside to draw water.

At the dinner table, Angie's mind was only on retiring to bed, but her mother insisted that the children bathed on Saturday nights so they'd be clean for Sunday church. Angie could feel herself falling asleep in the wash basin, the warm water soothing her tired body. But she felt good about what she had accomplished that day. *I'm not so little,"* she told herself, *"I can do all kinds of things to earn some money. I'll be able to get my yarn before winter sets in."*

After her bath, she dressed in her nightshirt, kissed her parents goodnight and dragged herself up the stairs, flopping onto her bed. Her mother came up behind her and covered her with her blankets.

Tucking her in, Faith said, "You did a very good job today. I'm very proud of how hard you worked."

"I'm so tired momma," Angie said quietly.

"I know," her mother said. "Try to be nice to Pearl, dear, alright?"

"I'm not going to be nice to Pearl," Angie responded with her eyes closed and beginning to drift off to sleep.

"Land sakes, my dear" Faith laughed gently. "You must get your stubbornness from your father."

"But stubbornness is a good thing, momma," Angie could barely be heard," Papa says stubbornness can make a body stand by his principles."

"Or worse," Faith stroked her daughter's head. "Just be sure to mix some sensibility in with that stubbornness or you may be standing all alone with your principles."

Angie was already asleep.

The next morning at the little neighborhood church, the pastor led the singing. The Owens always sat up front with the McKennas. When Pastor Johnson paused to ask if there were any testimonies from that congregation that morning, Angie sprung to her feet.

"I have something to say," Angie announced not realizing what a testimony was. She just knew it was a time for people who had something to say…to say it. "I am going to learn to crochet like my momma and I need a job so I can buy my yarn. I'll work hard for you. I know how to make beds, clean dishes, and even weed gardens. If you need an errand done or a chore done, I can do it for you."

She then promptly sat down with a grin on her face.

The congregation began to laugh, to Angie's surprise. *What was so funny?* she thought, and felt embarrassed, shrinking down in the pew. Her mother patted her on the knee and smiled as she whispered in her ear, "You said that exactly right, my dear."

"Then why did everyone laugh?" Angie whispered back.

"Because you did that so well, you made everyone happy," her mother quietly responded.

Angie knew that her mother was just being kind, and she still felt embarrassed.

After the church service while the Owens were shaking Pastor Johnson's hand, Elma and George walked up to Angie. George said, "I think we can help you earn some of that yarn. Come by our house in the morning and we'll find some jobs for you."

Angie beamed and thanked them.

"Oh Angie," Pearl called, "I have a job for you. You can clean up after our horses. A job you're fit for!" Cora, her mother laughed along with Pearl.

"No thank you," Angie responded, "I already have a job, a much better job!"

"Her parents are too poor to buy her some lousy yarn," Pearl said to her mother, "They're so poor, I bet Angie even has to work for the dirt on her face."

"Yes, it would seem so," her mother agreed and smiled at Faith.

"I don't have a dirty face!" Angie objected.

"Of course you don't," Elma tried to calm Angie. "Pearl is just making up lies."

"Never mind them," Faith said gently to Angie. "Evidently they have nothing better to do with their day than spread unhappiness."

"I'm glad she's not my mother," Angie said to Faith. "She's as mean as Pearl."

"Must be where Pearl learns it from," William added as he led them down the front steps of the church. "Let's go. It's time to go home for Sunday dinner. Your mother worked hard on it all morning."

"I'll beat you home" Billy challenged Angie as he got a head start on her, running ahead of the family.

"No you won't!" Angie called behind him and sped by him, beating him to the front door of their house.

William and Faith walked slowly behind. "It breaks my heart," Faith told William, "the way the Hubbards behave toward our family, especially toward Angie."

"We'll have to keep praying for them," William said.

"And praying for ourselves as well. My patience is running quite thin," Faith confided.

William held her hand as they walked up to the front door. "That's alright, my dear," he assured her. "A little patience goes a long way."

"I hope so." She shook her head as she followed behind the children into the house.

Early the very next morning, Angie rushed through her breakfast and ran to the McKenna house to begin her day of earning a few coins. She knocked at the door and waited for Elma to open it.

"My lands child," Elma remarked. "Do you know what time it is? I thought I was the only one who got up this early."

"I'm ready to work for you," Angie smiled.

"Well, alright," Elma said as she stepped out onto the porch. "Let's start right here, weeding the flower garden."

Angie moaned a little, but made sure Elma didn't hear her.

Elma walked past her and out to the yard. "Weeding," Elma pointed to her flower garden. "Lots of weeding to do. I'm afraid my garden gloves are too big for you Angie, but you can wear them if you'd like."

"That's alright," Angie knelt down onto the dark soil, "I'm not afraid to get my hands dirty."

Angie had been working in the garden for a little more than an hour when she heard a familiar voice beside her.

"What are you doing?" Pearl asked as she leaned over the three-foot fence.

"Working!" Angie answered as she went back to weeding Elma's garden, irritated that Pearl was standing there.

"Why?" Pearl asked.

"I'm earning money," Angie said through her gritted teeth.

"For yarn? That's silly. I wouldn't work for yarn!"

"I know **you** wouldn't," Angie looked up at her with disgust, "That's because you're too lazy."

"I'm not lazy, I'm rich, so I don't have to work. You're poor and sour about it," Pearl smiled.

"I am not sour, and you are too lazy!" Angie said as she stood to her feet.

"Take that back!" Pearl demanded.

"I will not!" Angie said as she came closer to Pearl, "I'm just speaking the truth! Why, you're so lazy, even the gypsies wouldn't want you!"

"You're so mean Angie Owens!" Pearl stomped her feet, "I'm going to tell my mother what you said and she's going to have your mother take you behind the woodshed for sure! And I'll be there to see it!"

"Not again! Girls, why do you always fight with each other?" Elma said as she came rushing out the front door.

"Why, you'd think you'd stay clear of each other they way you get on so. Now, Pearl, you run along home and no more of this bickering, you hear? And you'd better get back to weeding, Angie child. Lots to do before lunch time."

"Yes Mrs. McKenna," Pearl said sweetly and continued down the sidewalk while Angie knelt back down to resume working in the soil, still perturbed with Pearl.

Once Elma turned her back and began to return to the house, Pearl stopped suddenly, picked up a nearby rock, and threw it in Angie's direction, just missing her. Angie jumped up and glared her eyes at Pearl as Pearl ran quickly down the road toward her home.

Around noon, Elma sent Angie to the General Store with George's lunch.

"Well, look who's here!" George smiled when he saw Angie emerge through the door.

"I brought you your lunch," Angie said excitedly as she handed him the metal covered pan, "Where's daddy?"

"I sent him on a delivery," George said as he came around the counter.

"Hmmm, let's see what you've brought," George said as he took the pot and removed the lid, "Stew, chicken stew."

"And homemade bread!" Angie added as she showed him the loaf wrapped in a towel that had been under her arm.

"Well, this just won't do," George looked at Angie a little worried, "This is way too much food for me to eat. You'll just have to help me eat this."

Angie followed George to the little table by the shelves behind the counter and found a chair.

"After we eat, can I help you here in the store?" Angie asked, "Elma said it's getting too hot to work in the yard this afternoon."

George thought for a moment. "Well, I do believe the floor needs a good sweeping. With all the dust in the road, it gets tracked in here on a daily basis, and it's all I can do to keep up with it."

"I'll sweep the floor for you!" Angie said as her eyes wandered over to the domestic goods.

George caught her gaze and said, "I do believe we have some very nice yarns over there. You'll have to take some time before you go home today and make sure you have a good look at them."

Angie nodded her head as she took a bite of bread, and continued to look across the room at the yarns that sat on the shelves.

George smiled to himself and picked up a piece of bread to dip in his stew.

They were just finishing their meal when William came in the front door, surprised to see his daughter. "What are you doing here?"

"I brought George his lunch and now I'm going to help him clean the store."

"Oh, you are?!" her father grinned, "Are you sure you're not trying to take MY job?"

"No I'm not, daddy," Angie said as she grabbed the broom, "As soon as I get enough money for my yarn, I'm going to quit."

George and William laughed with each other at Angie's enthusiasm.

Angie swept and dusted the entire store, taking her time whenever she neared the yarn shelves, eyeing the colors and trying to decide which skein she would buy first.

George then said, "Time to go home so you'll have time to do your own chores. Take a look at the yarn on your way out and then return tomorrow."

"How long will it be before I can earn my yarn?" Angie asked.

George smiled, "Go ahead, and take a skein with you. You've earned one."

She ran over to the yarn shelves and spent time looking through each color.

"I'll take this one," she said as she showed George a blue skein, with a huge smile on her face.

"Very pretty," George nodded approvingly.

"Thank you!" Angie ran to her father who was helping a customer. She gave him a kiss on the cheek and ran out of the store hugging her skein of yarn close to her chest. She ran all the way home and could hardly wait to show her mother her day's earning.

Later that evening, Angie's mother said, "Mrs. Hubbard came to see me today."

Angie looked up at her mother as she helped dry the dishes from dinner.

"I hear you've been fighting with Pearl again," Faith said sternly.

"She just asks for it momma!" Angie protested, "And I don't like her."

"Now Angie, that's truly not very nice of you." her mother scolded.

"Well, she's not very nice either," Angie tried to defend herself.

"Maybe so, but what does the Good Book tell us to do when people treat us badly?" Faith asked her.

Angie didn't respond. She just continued to look at the dish she was drying.

"What does it say?" her mother gently insisted.

"I'm supposed to love my enemies," Angie replied. "And surely she is my enemy!"

"Then you'd best love her, despite yourself," Faith instructed.

"But why?!" Angie protested, "That just don't make no sense!"

"Doesn't make any sense, my dear. That just doesn't make any sense," her mother corrected her.

"Well, it doesn't!" Angie said looking up at her mother.

"Angie," her mother replied, touching the side of Angie's face, "we get more with sugar than we do with vinegar. Keep treating her with kindness and Pearl will eventually come around. You'll see. You may even become best friends."

"No I won't!" Angie looked horrified, "Not with her!"

"Angie?" her mother began, "will you at least try?"

After a long pause, Angie answered reluctantly, "I guess I could try, but it won't be easy."

"Yes, well, you'd better go to bed now," her mother instructed, "You have another early morning at Mrs. McKenna's house. You know she likes to get a fresh start on her day."

Angie set the last dish in the cupboard, set down the dish towel and ran upstairs to her bedroom.

"Treat her with kindness!" she muttered, "I'd rather kiss a skunk!"

The next morning, Angie ran to Elma's house to begin her day of earning a few more coins. She already knew which color of yarn she would choose next.

After working in the yard all morning, she went to the store with George's lunch, and once again, there was entirely too much food for George to eat on his own. Angie ate with George and her father, and then went about sweeping the floor.

****

The next few weeks went by quickly. School was soon to start. Pearl would come by the store with her friends and taunt Angie as she swept and cleaned shelves. Pearl was careful not to come by when Angie's father was there for fear of being disciplined by him. Once in a while George would chase them out of his store and they would run away laughing, calling Angie unkind names as they left. But Angie was sure to keep her mouth closed and her responses to herself. It was difficult for her, but her mother's words kept running through her mind.

Angie had now accumulated enough yarn to begin her crocheted blanket. She was bringing her last skein of yarn home with her that day.

"Mother, I have all the yarn I need now!" Angie yelled to the kitchen when she entered the house.

Her mother came out from the kitchen, wiping her hands on a kitchen towel. "That's wonderful, my dear. George and Elma have been very good to you, allowing you to work for them. Be sure to thank them."

"I did," Angie smiled as she laid the latest skein on top of the others.

"No, a very special thank you," Faith corrected her. "No one else has been so kind to you. You must be sure they know how much you appreciate their help."

"What should I do?" Angie asked her mother.

"You think on it," her mother smiled. "Something will come to you."

Angie then changed the subject, "Momma, can I borrow your crochet needle?"

"Yes, of course," her mother answered, "but you must take very good care of it and don't lose it. It's very difficult to replace."

"Can you show me how to crochet now?" Angie grew excited.

"After dinner and our chores are done, then I'll show you how to begin," Faith answered as she left to return to the kitchen. "Come and help me."

Anxious for her first lesson to begin, Angie was waiting for her mother in the living room. Billy was demanding Faith's attention and it was irritating Angie. She began pacing back and forth across the room, each minute seeming to stretch beyond Angie's patience.

"Alright," her mother said as she entered the room. "Let me get my crocheting needle and we can begin."

Angie sat down with her first skein of yarn on her lap, eagerly watching her mother. Faith sat down next to Angie and began to show Angie how to chain each stitch, and then she had Angie take over. Carefully counting until they had enough stitches to make a nice long blanket, Faith then took the yarn back to her lap and showed Angie how to crochet a beautiful design from each chain. She then handed the beginnings of the blanket back to Angie. After several attempts, and many minutes of Angie trying to master the needle as well as the stitch, Angie began to have success with her design.

"I wish I could crochet as fast as you," Angie told her mother as she struggled with each stitch.

"Don't worry about speed, that will come to you," Faith smiled, "The most important part of this blanket is what you put into it."

"What I put into it?" Angie looked confused.

"Yes. You need to fill it with blessings," her mother suggested. "Every time you make a stitch, you also add a blessing. That way, you'll have the most wonderful blanket of all, filled with blessings that will keep you warm."

"Blessings?" Angie was even more confused now.

"Make a stitch," her mother instructed and Angie did so, "Now that stitch is for love. Make another stitch."

Angie did so.

Her mother then said, "That stitch is for peace, and the next one is for patience, and the next for kindness. Do you understand?"

"I think so," Angie nodded. "And this one is for…umm… gentleness!"

"Very good!" Faith encouraged, "And when you can't think of another blessing to stitch into your blanket, then you just start over. You'll see. The blessings will make your blanket the most special blanket you've ever seen."

Angie smiled to herself as she added each stitch and each blessing. She spent most of the evening working on her blanket, completing almost two whole rows.

It's going to take a lot more work, and time, than I thought, Angie realized. *That's alright, just as long as I have it finished before the fair next year. I can do that!*

Each day Angie would rush home from school, complete her homework and work on her blanket once dinner was done and evening chores were completed. Billy would sometimes sit and watch her work on the blanket, but soon became bored with the repetitive stitches and listening to Angie whispering her blessings with each one. Sometimes Billy would help her come up with new blessings, but most of them were silly, like 'horses' and 'dogs' and 'flowers'.

"Those aren't blessings!" Angie would reprimand him. "Those are 'things'."

"Well, I like them," Billy reasoned, "They make me happy."

Angie just shook her head and continued to think of 'proper' blessings.

"Let's play a game," Billy suggested.

"Can't." Angie said, "I'm busy."

"But you're always busy," Billy objected, "You never have time to play with me anymore."

"Sorry." Angie responded.

"You're no fun anymore," Billy slid off the chair and headed out of the room.

Angie just continued her work on her blanket.

"Maybe you should take some time to spend with your brother," her mother said after overhearing the conversation and entering the room.

"Can't, momma," Angie responded, "I have to get this blanket done and it's going to take a lot of time."

"Yes, I know," her mother agreed, "But your brother needs some time as well."

Angie started to feel bad for her little brother and finally said, "Alright, I'll play a game with him."

She set down her yarn reluctantly and then went upstairs to find her brother.

When she walked into her brother's room, Billy looked up from his elementary book and his eyes grew big.

"Do you still want to play a game?" Angie asked.

Billy nodded his head.

Angie sat down on his bed and said, "Well, get the game of checkers."

The game was old and well worn, but brought many hours of enjoyment between the children. It was the only board game they owned and they took very good care of it. Tonight they would spend the rest of the evening laughing and challenging each other until mother called to them to get ready for bed.

That Sunday, in church, Angie had another testimony to share.

"I want to give a very special thank you to Elma and George McKenna," she announced loudly. "They helped me a lot so I could buy my yarn and make my blanket for next summer's fair."

She then promptly sat down and returned the McKennas' smiles. Her mother patted her on the knee and whispered, "Very nice, dear. Very nice."

****

The next few months went on fairly routinely. School, homework, dinner, dishes, and then working on her blanket.

One wintry December day, a few weeks before Christmas, Angie was putting on her coat, preparing to head home after school. Most of the other children had already left the little schoolhouse ahead of her.

"Are you still making that ugly blanket?" Pearl asked her. Betsy was standing at her side.

"It's not ugly," Angie returned her smirk. "And it's going to win a ribbon at the Boone County Fair next summer. Maybe even a blue ribbon!"

"If it's as ugly as your mother's blankets, they'll use it for the hogs to sleep on!" Pearl grinned.

The anger built up quickly inside Angie, and she forgot all about her mother's words to be kind to Pearl. She no longer wanted to 'kill Pearl with kindness', she just wanted to shut her up, and with that thought, she balled up her fist and hit Pearl with all the strength she could muster. Right in the stomach. Pearl bent over and fell to her knees. She screamed with more surprise than pain and yelled "Miss O'Brien! Angie Owens just hit me!"

Miss O'Brien came running to the back of the classroom.

What happened here?" their teacher asked as she helped Pearl to her feet.

"She hit me in the stomach!" Pearl exclaimed as she pointed at Angie.

"She did!" Betsy agreed, "I saw her!"

Angie just stood silent, surprised at her sudden reaction to Pearl's mean words.

"Are you alright?" Miss O'Brien asked Pearl.

"I don't think so," Pearl answered, "but I could be dying."

"Oh, I don't think **you are** dying," Miss O'Brien smiled, "but I think I'd better help you home. Angie, stay here. I want to talk to you when I get back."

Pearl and Betsy gave Angie long cold glares as they walked out of the classroom with Miss O'Brien. Pearl stuck her tongue out at Angie and then relished the thought that Angie was going to get her just rewards now.

Angie slowly sank in a nearby chair and began to think about the consequences that were sure to come. The minutes seemed to drag on forever. The longer she sat there, the more afraid she became. Tears began to stream down her face.

Momma was right, Angie thought, *Sticks and stones won't break my bones, and I should've been nice and just ignored Pearl. Now I'm in big trouble. I'll be punished for sure!*

It seemed like a very long time, but when Miss O'Brien returned to the classroom with an earful from Mrs. Hubbard, she was determined to put Angie in her place. Angie heard her enter the room behind her and began to sob.

The sight of the little girl's repentance softened Miss O'Brien's heart, and she quietly sat down next to Angie.

"Tell me what happened." She leaned next to Angie and looked into her face.

Between sobs and tears, Angie tried to say, "She said some really mean things about my momma and it hurt my feelings. She has no right to say those things. Pearl makes me so mad and my momma is good and kind and Pearl hates me and…"

"Alright," Miss O'Brien put her arm around Angie. "Calm down now. Let's talk about this, reasonably."

"I'm so sorry," Angie wailed, "I don't know why I did that. Momma told me to be nice to her. I should've listened to my momma."

"Yes, yes," her teacher agreed as she handed Angie her handkerchief, "It's good you realize the seriousness of this offense. Two wrongs don't make a right. Now listen to me."

Angie tried as hard as she could to stop crying and she tried to stifle her sniffles in the white cloth.

"Pearl is quite alright. But you did take the wind right out of her," Miss O'Brien told Angie. "Her mother is in such a snit and is demanding retribution."

"What's that?" Angie looked up at her teacher in fear.

"Punishment," Miss O'Brien gently told her.

Tears began to flow again from Angie's eyes.

"Now, now," her teacher said, "It won't be as bad as all that. But you must promise me that it'll never happen again!"

"It won't," Angie said, "I promise!"

"Alright then." The kindly teacher accepted her promise, "You'll need to stay after school for the next week and help me clean chalkboards and straighten the room. A good sweeping will also be in order."

Angie nodded her head and handed the handkerchief back to her.

"Good. Now get along home and let your mother and father know what went on here today."

"Yes, Miss O'Brien," Angie said as she rose to her feet, suddenly realizing that she was going to have to explain to her parents what she'd done. The dread was rushing through her little body and she wondered what would await her at home.

All the way home, Angie practiced what she was going to say to her parents, trying to justify her actions. Surely they'll agree with her.

When she entered her house, it was apparent that Mrs. Hubbard had been to see her mother again. Her parents sat in the living room waiting for her.

"Go upstairs," William instructed Billy. Billy jumped to his feet and obediently ran up the stairs to his room.

Fear crossed Angie's face as she stared at the sternness in her parents' expressions.

"She said some mean things about you momma!" Angie blurted out.

"You've gone too far this time." Her father was grieved.

"I didn't mean to hit her, honest!" Angie tried to explain "It's just that she made me so mad! I was trying to defend…"

"It doesn't matter," William stopped her. "You must learn that you cannot hit people, no matter who it is or what they've done."

Angie's eyes dropped to the floor and she realized that all her excuses were not going to ease her parents' anger.

"Sorry," was all Angie could say and the dread of punishment overwhelmed her.

"We've decided we'll have to take your yarn away from you. No more blanket for the fair next year."

"But daddy!" Angie protested, "I'm almost half done with it! I've been dreaming about the fair for months!"

"Sorry, Angie," her father responded, "but that's your punishment. Perhaps next time, you'll think twice about your actions before you get yourself into trouble."

Angie ran upstairs and threw herself on her bed, tears beginning to flow again.

Soon her mother called the children for dinner, but Angie didn't leave her bedroom. Her father appeared in her doorway, "Your dinner is on the table. Come on, we're waiting for you."

"I'm not hungry," Angie said with her head buried in her pillow.

"Suit yourself," William said. "But you'll still need to do the dishes after we're done eating." Angie then heard him walk down the stairs.

Angie beat her fists into her pillow and sobbed, *this has been the worst day of my life!*

The next day at school, Pearl grinned at Angie, "Did you get punished?"

Angie refused to say anything and walked past her, finding her place at her desk.

Pearl walked up to her. "Well, did you, you awful brat?!"

Again, Angie refused to acknowledge her and just stared straight ahead at the blackboard.

"You're being very rude," Pearl leaned over and said in Angie's ear, "Or are you just stupid?"

"Pearl," Miss O'Brien said as she entered the classroom, "find your seat. Class is starting now."

The teacher watched Pearl straighten herself and smugly walk away to the other side of the room. Miss O'Brien was a little disturbed to see Pearl's attitude and determined that she would keep a closer watch on Pearl from then on.

At the end of the school day, Angie was getting ready to leave when she noticed Pearl, Betsy, and Susanna waiting outside. She assumed they were waiting for her, to give her more grief.

Susanna was known as the local tomboy and loved to fight the best of the boys in class. Miss O'Brien also noticed the girls standing by the bottom of the steps as she glanced over Angie's head.

"Angie. Remember, you need to erase the chalkboards tonight," her teacher said, "and the broom sits over there."

Angie looked relieved and hung her coat back up, "Yes, Miss O'Brien. I'm sorry. I forgot."

She immediately went up to the blackboard and began to erase the day's lesson. Every few moments Angie would glance out the window to see if the girls were still standing there. By the time she picked up the broom, she was surprised to see the girls still outside, but by now they were beginning to shiver with the cold.

Serves them right, Angie thought, *May the weather be as cold as their hearts!*

She began to sweep the dirt across the floor. The next time she glanced out the window, she realized the girls had left. She stood for a moment, looking carefully out through the frosty glass, making sure that they had definitely gone.

Miss O'Brien was sitting at her desk, grading the day's papers, and watched Angie as she stared out the window.

"Are you quite done?" she asked Angie.

"Almost," Angie answered and began sweeping very quickly now.

"It'll be dark soon," Miss O'Brien remarked, "You'd best be on your way home now. You can finish sweeping after school tomorrow."

"Yes, Miss O'Brien" Angie said as she set the broom in the corner, grabbed her coat and books, and ran to the door.

"Good night, Miss O'Brien," Angie waved, "I'll see you tomorrow.

"Good night, Angie," Miss O'Brien smiled.

The days after that, Miss O'Brien kept a close eye on Pearl, and did what she could to keep her away from Angie.

Christmas was just around the corner and Angie was struggling, trying to find gifts for her family. She no longer asked about her blanket or her yarn. She knew it would be a long time before she would ever see them again. But she could not blame her parents.

It's my own fault for acting so stupid. Mother had warned me and I didn't listen.

She stayed close to her parents and the McKennas at church, and even Pastor Johnson seemed to watch out for her. There were always a few snide remarks from Cora after church service, but her parents would just smile and nod and be on their way.

Angie tried to follow their example, giving Pearl a quick smile and ignoring Pearl's icy stare.

"I'm proud of you," her mother said as they were setting the table for Sunday dinner.

Angie looked up at her with a confused look on her face.

"You've been acting very grown up lately, refusing to let Pearl make you angry. I'm very pleased and so is your father," Faith told her.

Angie smiled, "I'm trying very hard, momma."

"I know you are," her mother returned her smile. "I'm sure God is very pleased with you too. He's watching you, you know."

The smile left Angie's face as she began to contemplate the idea of God's judgment.

"Do you think He really is pleased with me?" Angie asked.

"Yes I do, dear," her mother told her, "I heard you pray for forgiveness when you said your bedtime prayers several weeks ago, and you're truly trying to make a change. That is all that can be expected of you."

Angie felt a sense of relief and a warm feeling flowed through her heart. And she felt her smile return to her face.

After school the next day, Miss O'Brien asked Angie to empty the wastebaskets. The trash needed to go out to the burn barrel.

As she was getting ready to dump the first wastebasket, she saw different colors of paper that had been tossed. She brought them back into the classroom and asked her teacher if she could have them.

"Of course," Miss O'Brien answered, "but what are you going to do with them?"

"I want to make Christmas presents out of them," Angie beamed.

"By all means," Miss O'Brien smiled, "Have as much paper as you need."

When she arrived home that late afternoon, she dropped her coat on the chair in the living room and ran up to her room. She then spread all the colored papers out on her bed.

"Angie," her mother called upstairs, "you left your coat on the chair again. Come back downstairs and put it away now. You know you can't leave it there."

Angie ran down the stairs, put away her coat and then returned as quickly as she could to her bedroom.

"Angie," her mother called again, "are you alright?"

"Yes, momma," she answered, "I just have a lot of homework to do."

She then separated all the colors and began to imagine a beautiful work of art, all made in a mosaic pattern. In her mind's eye, she saw her home, the little shed out back, the large maple tree out front and the fruit trees in back. Vegetables in the garden, flowers in the window boxes, and the neighbor's cat on their front porch. The cat was at their house more often than at its own home. The picture brought a smile to her face.

After dinner, while drying dishes, she asked her mother if she could borrow the pair of scissors.

"Scissors?" her mother asked. "And what are you making?"

"A Christmas present," Angie answered, "I can't tell you what it is."

"I see," Faith smiled. "Well, yes, in that case, you can borrow the scissors."

"Can you show me how to make paste then?" Angie asked eagerly.

"Tonight?" her mother asked.

"Tomorrow will be alright," Angie answered.

Her mother agreed and Angie returned upstairs. Angie's picture kept running through her mind, and she looked through the colored paper one more time before putting it away for the night.

After school the next day, Angie went out to the woodshed and found a wooden plank that had been cast aside. She was very pleased at the size and shape and wiped the dirt from it.

The Blanket of Blessings 53

When her father came home that night, she asked him if she could have the piece of wood and he nodded in agreement, not really paying attention to her request. He had many other things on his mind lately and barely had time for his family. The General Store had been busy with the holidays just a few days away and William was concerned about providing a good Christmas for his family.

Her mother kept her promise to show Angie how to make paste, and with a small bowl full of the newly made white concoction, Angie carefully carried it up to her room. With the scissors, Angie cut out different sized pieces of colored paper and began to fit them together on her piece of wood. Angie had an unusual talent for art and her grasp of creativity was growing with her age. She loved to let her imagination be expressed in her drawings. Besides working on her blanket, artwork was her favorite pastime and creating beautiful things with her hands gave Angie a great deal of self-worth. She dreamed of one day being as gifted as her mother.

****

Angie woke up to a very chilly morning, but there was a fire roaring in the fireplace and the smell of coffee coming from the kitchen. It was Christmas morning and she was excited to bring her gifts downstairs and set them under the small fir tree that her father brought home. She was fascinated with the handmade ornaments that hung on the thin branches. They represented years of memories, each one added one year at a time. This year, her mother added a new ornament that she crocheted from leftover yarn, a little white snowman with a blue top hat. Among the ornaments hung older ones that came from her grandparents, saved carefully by her mother. Each one had been wrapped in leftover paper from presents under the tree, and then stored in the old wooden chest in their parents' room. Angie loved to look at each one of them, imagining that each ornament had its own story to tell.

Billy was already in the kitchen, begging his parents to let him open his present. Angie went into the kitchen and sat down at the table.

"Merry Christmas," her father smiled at her as he sipped his coffee.

"Merry Christmas, daddy!" Angie answered, "Can we open our present now?"

Billy looked hopefully at his daddy and nodded his head in agreement.

"We're waiting for the McKennas" mother said as she sat down at the table, placing some freshly scrambled eggs before her family. "You know they join us every Christmas. Elma is bringing the dessert this year."

"But what about your apple pie?" Angie whined, "We always have your apple pie for Christmas. Elma's apple pie just isn't as good as yours."

"That's not very nice of you, Angie," her mother admonished her. "Elma works very hard on her pies, and would be very hurt if she heard you say that."

"But it's the truth, my dear," William chuckled and winked at his wife.

"Well, we'll eat it and enjoy it," Faith smiled.

"Yes, dear," William said as he passed the eggs to his wife.

The hour between breakfast and the McKennas' arrival seemed like an eternity to the children, patience not being one of their best virtues. Billy and Angie ran to the door to let the Mckennas come in from the cold, their arms holding gifts for under the tree.

Faith brought out fresh coffee for her friends and a few cinnamon rolls she had made especially for the holiday.

"This is a special treat," Elma said as she seated herself comfortably in front of the fire.

George smiled broadly as he carefully placed their presents among the others, being sure to let Billy spot which gift was his.

"Can we open gifts now?" Billy begged his father.

"Yes, yes, yes," William smiled wearily and finding a seat in the living room. "We can open our gifts now."

Billy was excited to receive his new coat from his parents, and the paper snowflakes his sister had made for him to hang in his window. But he loved the wooden carved horse that the McKennas gave him the most.

Angie waited anxiously for her parents to open her mosaic that she had made them, and her chest swelled up with pride when her mother and father ranted on and on about how beautiful it was.

"We'll hang it right here in the living room so everyone can enjoy it," her mother smiled.

Angie was so pleased with her gifts for her family, she had forgotten all about the ones that were sitting in front of her.

"Aren't you going to open your gifts, dear?" her mother asked Angie.

Angie was startled at the thought that she hadn't even opened her gifts yet, and then eagerly began to unwrap the first gift. The present was from her parents and held a modest, but pretty dress for school. Angie was excited and grateful to have a new dress to show off when she returned to school on Monday. She gave Billy a hug for the handmade sugar cookie he had decorated for her, but when she opened the McKennas' gift, she grew very quiet. Inside the long slender box was a crocheting needle. It was beautiful, made of smooth carved oxen bone that would last a lifetime. She suddenly set it down, said thank you to the McKennas and headed back upstairs to her bedroom, leaving her dress and cookie behind.

"What's wrong?" George asked William.

"I'm afraid she's being punished," William explained to George, "I had to take her yarn away from her a short while back. She got in a fight with Pearl Hubbard."

"Pearl Hubbard!" George remarked, "Well, if she got into it with Pearl Hubbard, I hope Angie got the upper hand in that fight."

"She may have gotten the upper hand," Faith smiled, "but she also got herself in a lot of trouble."

"She has to learn not to hit people," William explained, "and how to behave herself, no matter how others act."

"I don't think you fully understand how much Angie has taken off of that Hubbard girl. I've seen it, and I wanted to hit the little brat myself!" George added, "The girl needs a good spanking she does."

"Well, that's not how we handle things," William smiled, "but I have seen a lot of what goes on with Pearl and her mother, myself. Maybe I am being too harsh on Angie. I just want to make sure it doesn't happen again."

"I think she's learned her lesson, dear," Faith said gently.

William sat for a while, not saying a word, thoughts running through his mind. The room was oddly quiet, everyone watching William's face, except for Billy who was happily playing with his new wooden horse.

Without a word, William slowly rose to his feet and went up the stairs. Faith and the McKennas smiled to each other, knowing that this would be a better Christmas for Angie than she realized.

After making a short stop to his bedroom, William entered Angie's room, his arms holding the unfinished blanket and loose skeins of yarn. Sitting on her bed, Angie's eyes focused only on the blanket. Then she looked up into her father's eyes and was surprised to see a kindness she had not witnessed in his face for several months.

He sat down on the bed next to her, laying down the yarn and blanket in front of her, and said "I believe this is yours."

Angie didn't say anything. The surprise on her face said it all.

"Merry Christmas, Honey Bee," he smiled, gave her a kiss on her forehead, and then left the room.

Angie stared at her blanket. Her punishment was over. She would be able to have it finished in time for the fair in the summer. But why didn't it give her pleasure to have it back? She felt an overwhelming sadness come over her, along with guilt and displeasure. It brought back unpleasant thoughts of Pearl, of the disapproval from her mother and father and the shame she had brought upon herself. She rose from her bed, leaving the unfinished blanket where her father had placed it, went downstairs and joined the others for Christmas dinner.

As she retired that night, she thought about her blanket. *I need to work on it again, but not now. I don't want to work on it now. Maybe tomorrow. Maybe next week.*

****

CHAPTER THREE

The Accident

It had been several weeks after Christmas and Faith was concerned that Angie had not begun working on her blanket again. She noticed that Angie had placed her project in the corner of her room and there it sat untouched.

"Angie," her mother said as she entered her bedroom, "I noticed you're not working on your blanket. Is something wrong?"

Angie shook her head and went back to working on her homework.

"Don't you want to finish your blanket?" Faith inquired, insisting on facing the subject.

"You can finish it if you want," Angie said, not looking up at her mother.

"It's not my entry in the fair," her mother said sitting down on the bed next to Angie.

When no response came from Angie, Faith asked, "Dear, why have you lost interest in your blanket? I thought it made you happy."

"It makes me sad," Angie responded.

"For goodness sakes, why?" her mother was surprised at her answer.

Angie shrugged her shoulders and didn't answer.

"Because of Pearl?" Faith suggested.

Again Angie shrugged her shoulders.

"I see," her mother smiled, "Are you going to let Pearl Hubbard run your life? Are you going to let her take away your blue ribbon at the fair next summer? I think that would be a tragedy. Then Pearl would have gotten the best of you after all."

Angie looked up into her mother's eyes with a newfound interest.

"Don't let Pearl take away your blessings, my dear," her mother softly said, lovingly stroking the top of her head, and then rose from the bed and left Angie to ponder her words.

****

That Saturday in March was cold and rainy, as Angie triumphantly displayed her colorful blanket.

"It's finished!" she announced to her mother as she proudly held it up in the air to show off the blanket's completion.

"And what a blanket it is too!" Faith smiled broadly. "It reminds me of the story in the Bible, of Joseph's coat of many colors."

"It's my rainbow blanket," Angie said excitedly.

"It's your blanket of blessings," her mother reminded her, "and it needs just one more blessing to make it truly blessed."

Faith wrapped the blanket around Angie and said to her daughter, "May this blanket keep you forever warm." She then kissed Angie fondly on the cheek. Angie gazed up into her mother's face and a closeness she had never felt before flooded her heart.

The previous month, Angie's birthday had come and gone and suddenly she felt so much older, so much more mature. And with that new birthday, came more responsibility in the house. Making beds was added to her chores, along with helping her mother with washing the linens and clothing.

Angie ran upstairs with her new blanket and laid it out over her freshly made bed.

It looks wonderful! She thought to herself, *Surely, this blanket will fetch me at least a ribbon of some color! The blue one if I'm lucky!*

"Will you make me one?" Billy asked as he entered her room.

"But momma already made you a blanket," Angie said with a start.

"But I like all the colors," Billy smiled as he stroked the blanket with his hand.

"Alright," Angie said proudly, "I'll earn some more money this summer and make you one for Christmas if you'd like."

Billy smiled and hugged his sister with gratitude.

"Where is the blanket mommy made for you?" Billy asked.

"I put it in my hope chest for my little boy or girl. Someday, I'll wrap it around them and tell them all about our mother." Angie told Billy with a dreamy look in her eyes.

That night, as Angie climbed into bed, she carefully pulled the crocheted blanket up around her shoulders and enjoyed the warmth the blanket provided. She knew she should save her blanket for the fair, but she was too excited to wait. *It will still be beautiful when the fair arrives,* she reasoned.

****

The month of April started out unusually cold and the townspeople had become concerned for the crops that needed to be planted soon.

Angie had stayed after class to help Miss O'Brien clean the blackboards and straighten the desks. Angie enjoyed talking with her teacher and she volunteered to help Miss O'Brien faithfully every Friday.

Many months before, Miss O'Brien made a point to have a serious talk with Pearl and after that time, Pearl stayed away from Angie, at least while in the classroom at any rate. Other than the dirty looks and snide laughing with her girlfriends, Pearl reluctantly obeyed her teacher's instructions, which made life at school bearable for Angie.

As Angie waved goodbye, bolting out the schoolhouse door, Miss O'Brien hollered, "Have a good weekend, Angie. See you on Monday."

"Bye," Angie called back to her teacher as she ran down the dirt road, huddled in her wool coat and clamping her books to her chest. The cold chill in the air made her run a little faster than normal, thinking about the warm fire that would greet her at home.

As she quickly made her way through the living room door, she tossed her books on the sofa, stripped off her coat, and ran to the fireplace to warm her hands.

"Angie, did you put your belongings away?" her mother called from the kitchen. "You didn't toss them about did you?"

"I'm putting them away," Angie answered back so that her mother could hear her.

"Good girl. You have such a horrible habit of leaving your things lying around the house." her mother reminded her.

Angie picked up her coat and gloves and hauled her books upstairs. As she entered her bedroom and dropped her armload of items on her bed, she could hear her mother yelling up the stairs after her, "Do you have homework tonight?"

"Yes," Angie reluctantly answered, "but I have until Sunday to get it done."

"Sunday is a day of rest," her mother said, "Get it done tonight and you'll have tomorrow to play. I expect you to finish it before dinner."

"Yes, momma," Angie answered as she heard her mother return to the kitchen.

Billy ran into her room and jumped on her bed.

"Be careful of my blanket," Angie warned, "You'll get it dirty!"

"Do you wanna play a game?" Billy smiled.

"No, I have homework to do," Angie responded.

"Aw, come on, please? Just one game?" Billy begged.

Angie hesitated, "Alright, just one very short game."

Billy ran to his room and brought back the old worn board game. They played a game of checkers, then another and another, until mother called them for dinner.

The McKennas had come to join them for the evening, and more wild stories were told around the fireplace that night. The evening flew by and the next thing everyone knew, the McKennas were saying their goodbyes as they donned their coats. Billy had already fallen asleep and William was taking him upstairs to bed. Angie hugged Elma and George and then yawned as she realized she was getting sleepy too. She dragged herself upstairs, changed and prepared to climb under her warm blanket. Her parents had just tucked her in and her eyes were growing heavy when she realized that she had not done her homework, as promised. Her mother always made it a practice to go over her homework in the morning with her. The fear of not having the homework ready to show her mother made her waken. She listened for her parents to retire for the night and then quietly slipped out from under her covers.

She slowly and carefully made her way downstairs, not wanting to wake her parents. She found her way through the dark and into the living room, found the lantern from the living room table, hid it under her robe and brought it back to her room. There, she lit the lantern and pulled out her homework. The night was going by quickly as Angie worked feverishly to complete her papers. It was not too long before she signed her name to the work and set the completed homework down on the floor on the other side of the bed. She blew out the light and brought the lantern back downstairs, set it back down on the table and returned to crawl under her blanket, smiling to herself. *Now I won't get into trouble…again!"* Angie thought. She shut her eyes and felt herself drift off into dreamland…

"Angie! Angie! Wake up!"

Angie slowly drifted from her dream back into reality. She opened her eyes and saw only darkness.

"Angie! Wake up now sweetheart!"

Before she could get a full picture of what was happening, her father was wrapping her up in her crocheted blanket and quickly lifted her from her bed.

"What's the matter?" she asked as her father rushed her down the stairs.

"The house is on fire," he answered and then carried her outside, placing her down next to the safety of a big tree by the road. Angie watching the burning of their home as it lit up the night sky.

"Where's momma and Billy?" she asked as her father knelt beside her.

"I don't know," William was alarmed, "They were supposed to be right behind me. Stay here, I'll go get them. Stay here! Do you hear me?"

Angie nodded, wrapped her blanket tightly around her, and watched her father run back into the burning house.

Her eyes kept searching for them to come out, but they didn't emerge. After what seemed an eternity, she got to her feet to go after them, but her father's words kept running through her mind and she hesitated. Suddenly voices from down the road caught her attention. Neighbors were emerging out of the darkness. She ran to them and pointed to the house, saying "My momma and daddy and brother are in there!"

Several neighbors ran past her and tried to get into the house but the flames drove them back. Others stood beside her and muttered to each other, women holding hands over their mouths. Men were shaking their heads and wondering what to do.

"Help them!" Angie cried, "Help my family!"

"There's nothing we can do," one man told her. "The fire is too hot. We can't get near it."

Angie started to run toward the burning house, but someone caught her arm and stopped her. It was George. He held her fast as she screamed for someone to help. Elma grabbed Angie and held her tightly against her chest. As she knelt in the grass, she got Angie to look straight into her eyes, "Child, you must come with me. You can't go in that house. You will perish too."

"Perish?!" Angie said. "What does that mean?"

"Your family has gone to see Jesus, child." Elma stressed the words, "They are no longer here in this world."

"No!" screamed Angie, "that's not true!"

"Yes, child, it is true. Come with me now. There is nothing here you can do." Elma turned Angie away from the blazing sight.

Angie looked stunned. She felt as if she was in a daze and knew this was only a horrible nightmare that she would soon awaken from. She sensed she was floating down the road, not really understanding the reality of it all. George and Elma were on each side of her, speaking gently to her, but Angie couldn't recognize the words coming from their mouths. Her mind was filled with confusion and unbelief.

As she was being tucked into a bed of down, she knew she would wake in the morning and all of this nonsense would be gone. She would be back home in her own bed with Billy laughing in his room next to hers, and wonderful smells coming from the kitchen. She knew it would turn out that way. She just knew it, and the comfort of the thought helped her drift back to sleep.

****

The next morning, Angie woke up to a strange room, a strange bed, and a feeling of dread in her heart. The nightmare, that terrible nightmare, it was over, so why wasn't she in her own bedroom. She slowly pulled back the blankets and saw her crocheted blanket of blessings laying on top of the comforter next to her. It was dirty and smelled like smoke. She quickly dropped it back on the bed and found her way into the living room. She realized she was in Elma and George's house. She had been there many times before for dinner with her family.

She heard someone rustling around in the kitchen and peered in to see Elma busily making biscuits.

Elma suddenly turned to see Angie. "Good morning, child. Come in and get some breakfast while it's hot."

Angie wandered in and sat down at the table.

"Where is everyone?" Angie asked her.

"Why, George is at the store, my child," Elma replied.

"No," Angie objected, "Where is my momma and daddy? And Billy?"

Elma slowly set down her hot pad and came over to the table to sit beside Angie.

"Angie," Elma began, "do you remember what happened last night?"

Angie fearfully shook her head 'no'.

"There was a terrible fire…," Elma began.

"No," Angie kept shaking her head, "no there wasn't. It was all a dream. A really bad dream!"

Elma placed her hands on top of Angie's and she wept for the little girl who seemed to feel nothing.

The next few days went by in a gigantic blur for Angie. She knew there were people coming and going, words of sympathy that didn't make much sense, and her movements were automatic, as if they were chores that needed to be done.

"Come, my child," Elma said as she helped Angie with her coat, "it's time for us to go." Elma put her hand on Angie's shoulder and guided her out the door. People were waiting outside, lots of people, and among them was the pastor. Pastor Johnson led the procession down the road, with Elma, George and Angie directly behind him. Angie was beginning to realize what was happening and where they were going, but she tried to push the knowledge from her mind.

As the procession reached the graveyard, Angie saw three freshly covered gravesites, with her parents' and brother's names on the wooden crosses that stood above them. She could not take her eyes away from the crosses, no matter how badly she wanted to.

Pastor Johnson was speaking words, lots of words, but the memories of three nights ago began to run through Angie's mind. The sound of a hymn was beginning to flow through her ears, soft and sweet. *Why are they singing?* Angie asked herself; *Don't they realize something terrible is happening here? You sing when you're happy, not now, not here!*

She looked up at the adult's faces, tears streaming down their faces, all so somber and grieving. She wanted to run away, but her feet refused to move. Then the pastor was beginning to walk away, where others joined him, shaking his hand and wandering on down the road, away from Angie. Away from the three crosses that bore her family's names. *Where is my name?* she thought, *I should have died too. I want to be with them!*

Angie was suddenly startled when she realized that Pearl had marched up to her and said, "I'm sorry to hear about your family." Her mother, Cora, looked proudly at her daughter's declaration of sympathy.

Angie turned her gaze back at the crosses.

"Did you hear me? I said I was sorry about your family!" Pearl insisted. "Aren't you going to say something?"

"There's nothing to say," Angie turned to look at her.

"Come along, dear," Cora said, "She's obviously just plain rude. She was probably never taught any decent manners as you were. Those Owens always were an inferior family."

"Now you mind your tongue" Elma scolded Cora as she wrapped her arm around Angie's shoulder. "The Owens were the finest people around this town. Don't you go talking about people you hardly knew. Why did you come here anyway?"

"To pay my respects of course," Cora answered in surprise, "After all, it's the polite thing to do. I was brought up with the proper instruction, unlike some people here."

"Well, when you're ready to pay some PROPER respects," Elma began, "you can come back. Now please leave us in peace."

"Well!" Cora snorted, "I was only trying to show my concern for the less fortunate and this is what I get for it! Come along Pearl, I'm sure we can find better company than what is here!"

"Don't count on it" Elma uttered under her breath.

Elma turned to Angie, knelt down and looked her straight in the eyes. "Angie, things are going to be very different now, but the good Lord is always with you. You're a strong little girl and you've got your father's hard work ethics and your mother's good nature. Let these qualities be your stronghold to get you through these bad times. Be brave and always remember to say your prayers every night when you get ready to close your eyes. Those prayers will see you to better days."

Angie wrapped her arms around Elma and the tears began to flow. The sweet relief of mourning began to release itself in the little girl who felt left all alone.

For the next few days, Angie didn't feel like doing anything. She just laid in her bed and stared blankly out the window. Thoughts of the fire and that fateful night would revisit her over and over again. Was it her fault? Did she forget to blow out the lantern? Was it the fire in the fireplace? Was it not completely out when they retired? The idea of it possibly being her fault that her family was gone was almost more than she could bear, and she tried as hard as she could to push the guilt from her mind.

Elma had allowed Angie time to mourn, but now felt it was time for Angie to start recovering. Elma knocked at the guest room door, peered in and quietly walked over to Angie, sitting herself down on the bed next to the pale little girl.

"My goodness child, you are looking a might peaked. You need to get outside and get some sun."

"I don't feel like it," Angie quietly muttered.

"I know you don't, but I love you and I'm not about to see you waste away," Elma told her, "Now get yourself up, get dressed and come have something to eat. Then we're going to walk to the store and get some flour. I want you to help me make some bread."

"I don't know how," Angie objected.

"I'll teach you," Elma assured her, "Now come on, no more excuses. Up with you and hurry yourself. Can't wait all day. Daylight's a-burning."

George and Elma had bought a few necessary clothes, a coat, and a pair of shoes to replace what Angie had lost in the fire. Elma pulled them out of the closet and set them on the bed.

"I'll wait for you in the living room. Don't be long," Elma insisted, "It takes a might of time to bake bread."

Angie held Elma's hand as they strolled quietly down the dirt road toward the General Store.

"Child, you hardly ate anything," Elma said, concerned. "You're gonna make yourself sick if you aren't careful."

Angie shrugged her shoulders.

Elma smiled and said, "Look, see Mrs. Snell's flowers? Her garden is the most beautiful around. Even the birds must think so. You can hear them just singing away in her big tree over there."

Angie looked where Elma was pointing, but then turned her stare back down to the road.

As they entered the store, George looked over at them and remarked, "Well, there's my two favorite girls. What brings you to see me today?"

"We came to bring you your lunch and to buy some flour," answered Elma. "We're going to make bread today."

"Well, since you came all the way to see me," George smiled at Angie, "I've got something special for you." He lifted the lid off one of the candy jars on the counter and held it in front of Angie. "Well, go on. Take a piece," George encouraged her.

Angie reached in and took a piece of peppermint and quietly said 'thank you'.

"Oh come on, you can do better than that!" George joyfully remarked. "Give me a smile…come on…give me a big smile."

The emptiness of not seeing her father at the store was a painful reminder of the past week, but Angie tried to put a smile on her face as she looked up at him.

"See, I knew there was a smile hiding in there somewhere. You should see how pretty your face is when you smile, and how your eyes sparkle, "George remarked, "Why, I think the stars couldn't outshine those eyes of yours!"

Angie's smile grew a little wider and she lifted the bag of flour for Elma and offered to carry it home.

That night, as George, Elma and Angie gathered at the dinner table, Angie thanked Elma for teaching her how to make bread.

"It's really good," Angie smiled at Elma.

"Yes, I must say, you're even a better cook than me," Elma smiled back. "Perhaps we'll try something new tomorrow."

"I'd really like to learn how to cook and we can make something new every day, and maybe we can even bake cakes and cookies and pies…" Angie's voice trailed away and she was deep in thought again, remembering her mother's blue ribbon pies.

"And your pies will be absolutely the best in the county," Elma smiled as she touched Angie's hand, "Just like your mother's pies."

"Elma," Angie started, "what will become of me now?"

"Angie, my child," Elma said gently, "you are to stay with us. We'll do our very best to care for you as your parents would have wanted us to." George nodded in agreement.

Angie smiled at Elma, jumped from her chair and embraced Elma around the neck. "Thank you, Elma. I'll be a good girl, I'll clean and learn to cook, and I'll do my very best!"

Then she ran to George and hugged him, "I'll sweep your store and clean your shelves for you. You'll see! I'll make you proud of me."

"We're already proud of you, Angie sweetheart," George whispered in her ear.

Angie's days became very routine. She had returned to school, where Miss O'Brien watched over her with a very protective hand. She would then run to the store and help George with the cleaning, and once in a great while, George let her help the customers. If he saw Pearl approach the store with her friends, he was careful to ask them their business, wait on them personally, and then usher them out of the store as quickly as possible. It was not the time for Angie to have to deal with them on her own, not for a while anyway.

George and Angie would stroll back to the house together and George would tell her all the jokes and tales he had heard at the store that day. She loved to listen to George's tales. It reminded her of the days when she was with her family and everyone would laugh well into the night. The familiar feelings would flow back and made her feel secure. Even the congregation at church always looked forward to Angie coming through the door, and made her feel like family, much to Pearl's displeasure.

The days started to warm and Angie's coat had been replaced by a brand new sweater Elma had knitted for her. As Angie entered the yard, she saw her rainbow blanket hanging from the laundry line. She walked over to it, touching the still damp yarn. It smelled clean and the colors were bright again. She smiled as she remembered the blessings her mother taught her; love, peace, truth, caring, gentleness, meekness, kindness....*Someday I'll teach my little girl how to make a Blanket of Blessings and tell her about my mother.*

****

CHAPTER FOUR

The Letter

The loneliness of Angie's days were filled by Elma and George's kindness. She had grown to love them as if they were her own family. It was the middle of July when George stopped by the post office on his way home. Angie was by his side.

"I hear we have a letter," George spoke to John.

John Page, the local Postmaster, smiled, turned and searched behind him, "Here it is!"

After George received the letter, he read the return address and his hand began to shake.

"Who's it from?" Angie asked curiously.

"Family, my sweetheart," George smiled to her. "It's from family."

"Is it your brother?" Angie questioned him again.

"We'll have to open it when we get home and find out!" George laughed.

Angie was curious why he wouldn't open it now, but kept quiet about the letter until they arrived at the house.

"Elma!" Angie called, "We have a letter!"

"Oh, and who is it from, George?" she asked as she set down her knitting.

"From Charity, my dear, "George answered Elma, "From Charity and Benjamin Baker."

The names sounded familiar, but Angie had not heard them in a long time and she was struggling to remember who they were.

"It's your aunt and uncle, Angie," Elma's face became very serious. "They've written us a letter."

George looked at Elma, "Well, open it Elma. What do they have to say?"

Elma's fingers fumbled as she tried to open the envelope.

"Dearest George and Elma," Elma began, "This letter comes to you with all best wishes for your health and happiness. Our deepest gratitude to you for caring for our dearest Angie these past months. I regret that the word of my dear sister's passing, and that of William and little William took so long to reach us. I am pleased to hear that little Angie is still with us.

As her closest living relatives, Benjamin and I are sending for Angie with the intent that she come to live with us in Sacramento. I have arranged for her to join the wagon train heading west, leaving Independence, Missouri on August 15th, 1854. She will be traveling in the accompaniment of the Smith brothers whom we've hired to ensure she arrive safely into our hands before winter arrives in the mountains.

Please ensure that Angie be ready for travel on August 11th for her journey to Independence. A Western Union cashier's check will be waiting for you at the local office on August 1st. This check will allow you to get Angie whatever traveling items she will require, as well as monies for her to use along the way for necessities. Again, we send our deepest appreciation for your care of our niece. Thank you very kindly, Charity and Benjamin Baker."

Elma slowly set down the letter and looked up at Angie. Tears were forming in the little girl's eyes. The silence in the room was deafening as Elma and George began to process the meaning of the letter in their minds.

Suddenly, Angie jumped up and ran to Elma, burying her head in Elma's lap.

"Please let me stay with you Elma, I'll be good. I can help you in your store and work in your yard. I can pull your weeds and plant your flowers. I can clean your house and I'm good at washing and drying dishes and I'll even make my bed every day, I promise" Angie pleaded.

Elma stroked the little girl's head and said quietly, "Child, there's nothing we can do. Your aunt and uncle have the right to have you live with them. They are family. We are not."

"But I don't know them!" Angie tried to reason, "I haven't seen them since I was a little girl."

"I know your Aunt Charity and your Uncle Benjamin," Elma continued, "They're good people. They used to live here in town before they headed west for the gold rush five years ago. Don't you remember them?"

Angie thought hard for a moment or two and then nodded her head.

"Your aunt is so much like your mother. You'll be very happy living with her. And your Uncle Benjamin is very kind hearted and will treat you well," Elma smiled as Angie looked up into her eyes.

"I suppose so," Angie quietly agreed, "But I love you. I'll miss you and George. What if I never see you again?"

"Well," Elma said, "we just won't think about that now, will we. Let's just enjoy each day we have together and make the best of it, shall we?"

"Alright," Angie said, "But I don't want to leave here."

"Perhaps it is for the best, sweetheart," George added, "Perhaps the Good Lord knows you need a fresh start, away from here. Someplace new where you can see new things and make new friends, and get to know your aunt and uncle again."

Angie thought about his words but did not respond. Again, it was silent in the room.

Finally Elma broke the silence, "Well, dinner's ready. Let's go eat our meal together."

"I'm not very hungry," Angie quietly told Elma.

"Well, I suppose no one is, but let's go and try to have a bite or two anyway," Elma encouraged them, "Our bodies still need the nourishment."

After Angie had retired for bed, George and Elma could hear her crying.

"That poor little girl has cried more tears in the last few months than any child should cry in a lifetime," Elma said to George.

"Let's hope she won't have a reason to cry anymore once she reaches Sacramento," George agreed.

"One month," Elma said quietly. "We'll only have her with us for one more month. She has become like our own daughter. How will we ever let her go?"

George held Elma's hand, "I don't know, Elma dear, but somehow we have to let her go."

Elma nodded and her heart began to ache.

The following day, while Angie was walking to the store with George's lunch, Pearl ran up behind her and yelled "Angie! Wait! Angie!"

"What do you want Pearl?" Angie turned to face her.

"I heard you're going to California soon!" Pearl said excitedly.

"I suppose so," Angie answered as she returned to walking toward the store. Pearl struggled to keep up with Angie's fast pace.

"Are you sad to go?" Pearl asked.

Angie didn't answer.

"It's a shame you have to move away to such an uncivilized part of the country, but then, you'll probably fit in better there anyway. Columbia is too sophisticated for you. Everyone says so."

"And who is everyone? Your family?" Angie asked.

"Yes, and everyone else as well," Pearl smiled.

"It's always 'everyone else', isn't it," Angie remarked, "Well, sometimes the most uncivilized are the wisest. **Everyone** says so."

And with that, Angie entered the front door of the store. Pearl knew better than letting George see her with Angie and so she started on her way down the road.

"Oh Pearl," Angie stuck her head out the door and waited for Pearl to turn around. "I won't miss **you**," Angie yelled and stuck her tongue out at Pearl, pulling her head back inside the store before Pearl had a chance to react.

****

The next three weeks went by entirely too quickly, spent mostly preparing for Angie's trip west and receiving good wishes from neighbors and friends. Elma spent a lot of time teaching Angie how to knit so that she'd have something to pass the time on the long trip to California. George and Elma received the cashier's check as promised and bought Angie the clothes and boots for the long trip, along with some yarn so she could knit herself a shawl for the autumn that was coming.

It was the night before the Smiths were due to arrive, Angie's last night with the McKennas. No one spoke during dinner and hardly any food was touched. A sadness filled the room and the knowledge that this was their last night together grieved all three.

"We have something for you," Elma smiled to Angie. "Something for you to remember us by."

She rose from the table and left the room, returning in just a few minutes.

"Here you are," Elma said, handing Angie a paper wrapped package with string tied around it.

Angie hesitated, and then took it from Elma's outstretched hand. George was sitting at the table and smiling as well, anxious for Angie to open it. Angie slowly and carefully untied the string and peeled back the paper, careful not to tear it. There under the wrapping was a brand new black leather Bible.

Angie looked up at them, smiled and said, "For me?"

"Look inside the first page," Elma encouraged.

Angie opened the book where she saw a handwritten message. It read: "To our dear Angie. May God go with you on this new adventure and may He bring you safely back to us someday. Love, George and Elma McKenna."

Angie hugged them both, "Thank you. I've always wanted my own Bible. This is wonderful. And I **will** come back to you someday. I promise!"

George and Elma laughed. "Yes, I'm sure you will." George said.

The next morning, Elma came into the living room carrying Angie's travel bag and blanket. Angie looked at her blanket and said, "It's so sad I won't be able to enter my Blanket of Blessings in the county fair like I promised my momma."

"Enter it in the Sacramento fair next year, my child. It will be just as worthy of a blue ribbon there," Elma assured her.

Suddenly, a knock came on the front door. No one wanted to move to answer it. Finally, George stood up from his comfortable chair and walked to the door, opening it to two older men looking somewhat ragged.

"Howdy. My name's Homer Smith and this here's my brother, Elmer Smith. Can't remember our birth name so we just go by Smith."

"You can't remember your real name?!" Elma remarked in surprise.

"Our ma and pa left us a long time ago. Headed for better places, I guess. We were told we was too much trouble to take along, so we been scrappin' in the streets ever since. Doin' a pretty good job of it too. Got us this far!" Homer smiled showing a missing side tooth. Elmer nodded in agreement.

"Well, you had just better take good care of our little Angie, here, "George warned them, "Make sure she reaches her Aunt Charity and Uncle Benjamin safe and sound or I'll be sure to hunt you down and make it right!"

"Now dear," Elma touched George's arm. "I'm sure it'll be alright," she said reassuringly as she invited them into the house.

"Well, I'm not so sure!" George responded giving the two brothers a suspicious glare.

Homer felt very uncomfortable. "We gotta get on the road if'n we're goin'ta catch that wagon train."

"Yes, yes..." Elma agreed, "We have her belongings right here."

Elma turned and said "This is our little Angie." Angie slowly rose from her chair and hesitated to meet the two men standing in front of her.

"Well, ain't she a pretty little thing," Homer smiled at Angie, "We're gonna get on just fine, ain't we?"

Angie looked up at him but her face remained expressionless.

"Don't you worry," Homer shook George's hand, "We'll take good care of her. You'll see. You'll be hearin' from her aunt and uncle in no time."

"I'd better," George said as he stared Homer in the eyes.

"Get the little lady's baggage, Elmer," Homer said as he started out the door. Elmer did so and followed closely behind him.

"I don't want to go," Angie clung to Elma, "Please don't make me go."

"You know we would keep you if we could," Elma told Angie as she knelt beside her. Looking into the little girl's blue eyes, Elma tried to be brave, but it was breaking her heart as well. "Your Aunt Charity is a wonderful woman, both sweet and kind. She's looking forward to you coming to live with her. You'll have a wonderful life there, much better than here. Now go, and mind your manners. Be a good girl and make us proud of you."

"I will" Angie struggled to stop crying.

"Go!" Elma encouraged her.

As Angie slowly disappeared through the door, Elma ran to the door to wave goodbye. George was outside giving Homer and Elmer last-minute warnings.

George helped Angie into the back of the wagon, with Homer and Elmer waiting for her on the front bench.

"Giddy-yap!" Homer called out as he slapped the reins on the back of the mules. The rickety old wagon began its slow journey away from the McKenna house. Angie waved goodbye from the back, tears still streaming down her face. George and Elma waved until she was out of sight and then Elma collapsed to the floor, breaking down and sobbing with no control left. George knelt down to hold her and his tears mingled with hers.

Angie lay down in the back of the wagon. Her thoughts turned to God. *Now I lay me down to sleep, I pray the Lord my soul to keep. Please watch over me throughout the night, and wake me with your morning light.*

****

CHAPTER FIVE

The Visit

Angie realized she had fallen asleep with the rattling of the wagon. She rubbed her sleepy eyes and gazed about her. Sitting up, she spread out her blanket and wrapped it around her. She wasn't cold. She just needed to feel comforted. She felt tears begin to form in her eyes again, but she fought them back.

I won't cry, she told herself, *I'm strong like my daddy. I won't cry!!*

Other than her blanket, everything surrounding her looked foreign. She examined the worn canvas of the old prairie wagon above her and the rusty lantern that swung from the wooden ribs that held the canvas from falling. The old wooden planks that held the wagon together smelled strange and the rattling of the wheels over the road sounded even stranger. She could hear the men talking to each other from the front of the wagon, but she didn't pay any attention to what they were saying. She wasn't sure she liked them anyway.

Pulling her knees up to her chest, she wrapped her arms around them, and then laid her head down on top of her knees. Angie wondered why all this had happened to her. Why did she have to go to California to live with relatives she didn't really know? Why couldn't she stay with Elma and George where she felt safe? Why did her family have to die?

She reached over to her bag and pulled out the Bible Elma had given her. As she ran her hand over it, she felt a wave of peace flow over her and she let the words inside the book calm her fears. She couldn't understand many of the words that the scriptures held, but the ones she could read helped her relate to her past, to her parents reading to her in the evenings, to their soft and gentle voices, to better times.

The wagon rounded the corner of the road and headed down a side dirt trail that was well rutted. As it came to a stop in front of an old farmhouse, Homer yelled back at Angie, "We'll be stayin' here for the night!"

Angie peered out at the farmhouse and the woman who came out the front door. She was short and a bit round with gray streaked hair and a face that was beginning to wrinkle.

"Why, Homer and Elmer!" she smiled as she held out her arms to them, "It's so good to see you. What in the world are you up to?"

The brothers jumped down from the wagon and she gave them both a big hug.

"Howdy, Gertie." Homer answered, "We here's just passin' by on our way to meet up with the wagon train in Independence. Hopin' we can spend the night here."

"'Course you can, 'course you can," Gertie answered. She noticed Angie watching her from inside the wagon and asked "Well, who's your traveling companion?"

Elmer helped Angie down out of the wagon, "This here's a Miss Angie Owens. We been takin' her to Sacramento to meet up with her aunt and uncle."

"Well," Gertie smiled at Angie, "isn't that nice. Are you hungry, girl?"

Angie nodded her head, a little hesitantly.

"We all is hungry," Homer agreed.

"It'll take me a moment or two to fix up some flapjacks. They ain't much, but they're filling!" Gertie said as she headed back up the old creaking steps to her front door. She turned and said, "Come on Miss Angie Owens, come make yourself comfortable."

As Angie entered the old farmhouse, she looked around at the bare necessities that laid about the room. The windows were open to allow the cool evening air clear all the stuffiness away and allow the crispness in.

Gertie was firing up the stove and talking about how long it had been since she saw the Smith brothers.

"I've known those two for going on 8 years now," Gertie told Angie. "They used to work for my husband, caring for our horses and mules."

"Speakin' of mules," Homer said as he entered through the door, "we'll need to buy two or three mules from ya."

"Buy?!" Gertie looked surprised, "You have money, Homer?"

"I surely do," he smiled and threw some paper money on the table.

"Don't wanna know where you got it from," Gertie laughed, "long as I can spend it!"

"How's life treatin' ya, Gertie?" Elmer asked as he came in from putting the mules away for the night and sitting himself down at the small kitchen table.

"Could be better," she answered as she began frying the flapjacks. "Been a might lonely here these past couple of years without my Henry."

"He was a mighty good man," Elmer offered.

Gertie nodded, "None finer."

"Maybe I'll marry ya myself,' Elmer smiled. "On our way back through, I'll stop and see if you're obligin'."

"Elmer Smith, you're just an old fool!" laughed Gertie.

Angie was amused by the banter between Elmer and Gertie, but Homer was not.

"Stop actin' like an old fool, Elmer!" Homer scolded. "You're embarrassin' us all!"

"Miss Angie Owens," Gertie said as she set a plate of flapjacks down in front of the little girl, "you can share my bed tonight. Been a long time since I had someone to keep me company."

"I have a mattress in the wagon," Angie objected, not wanting to be that close to Gertie.

"Suit yourself," Gertie smiled and then placed a plate of flapjacks in front of Elmer.

After dinner, Angie sat at the table and watched the other three play poker. She didn't understand the game and was growing increasingly bored with the whole evening. Her eyelids were getting heavier and heavier and her head began to nod.

"Homer and Elmer Smith!" Gertie laid down her cards. "This little girl's falling asleep. It's way past her bedtime and you're keeping her up!"

"One more game," Elmer suggested.

"After you put her to bed," Gertie agreed.

As Elmer escorted Angie out to the wagon, she noticed the two pup tents set up next to the wagon and realized she would have the wagon all to herself. She was grateful for that and allowed Elmer to lift her up into the back of the wagon.

"Crawl into bed, missy," Elmer said. "We'll be out in a bit."

"Good night, Elmer," Angie said as she made her way under her blanket.

She heard the front door slam as Elmer went back into the house and then the familiar sounds of the night caught her attention. She could hear the crickets nearby, and the hoot of an owl far away. Once in a while, she heard a muffled laugh from inside the farmhouse, and the wind began to blow through the trees over the wagon. The rustling leaves began to lull her to sleep and the warmth of her blanket sank her deep into her dreams.

"Get up, girl!" Homer yelled outside the wagon. "Time to eat and then we gotta be on our way!"

The morning had come so soon. Angie felt like she had barely closed her eyes and it was time to wake up. She stretched and then searched for her brush to work the snarls out of her hair.

As she entered the house, Gertie smiled and said, "There's some water over there for washing up." She was pointing to a basin on the table. "I've laid you out some lye soap and a towel."

"Thank you," Angie said as she walked over to the table.

"You're a mighty quiet girl," Gertie observed, "Don'tcha talk much?"

Angie shook her head.

"Oh, that's alright," Gertie said, "I don't think I said much at your age either."

Angie eyed Gertie with curiosity as Gertie laid more flapjacks down in front of her for breakfast.

"We've all had breakfast," Gertie told her, "I imagine you'll be on your way soon."

Gertie then went outside where Homer and Elmer were hooking up the mules.

"I've decided we need three more mules. How much ya want for 'em?" Homer asked her.

Gertie thought for a moment. "Fifty US dollars each."

"Fifty dollars?!" Homer exclaimed.

"That's a right fair price," Elmer told him.

Gertie held her smile.

"Humph!" Homer grunted, "Long as I have my pick."

"Deal!" Gertie held out her hand.

Homer pulled out a small bag from his pocket and placed the coins in Gertie's hand.

"Help yourself!" Gertie said as she pointed to the corral. "But only three mind you!"

As Homer tied the three newly purchased mules to the back of the wagon, Elmer had gone back into the house to get Angie.

"You done eatin'?" Elmer asked.

Angie nodded and rose from the table. She collected the dirty dishes and took them over to the counter by the stove.

"Well, ain't that nice," Gertie said as she entered the house. "You're quite the little helper. Could sure use you around here."

"I'm going to Sacramento," Angie said quietly, "to live with my aunt and uncle."

"So I hear," Gertie smiled, "Come give me a hug before you go."

Angie hesitantly gave Gertie a little hug and then backed away quickly.

Elmer gave Gertie a big hug and lifted her into the air. "I meant what I said Gertie," he smiled, "I think I'm gonna have to marry ya when I come back through."

Gerta laughed. "Well, we'll just have to see about that Elmer Smith. We'll just have to see about that!"

As Elmer lifted Angie into the back of the wagon, Gertie came running out of the farmhouse with a tattered basket in her hand.

"Wait!" she called, "I have some jerky and some leftover flapjacks for you."

Homer was already sitting on the front bench with the reins in his hand. Elmer walked over to Gertie as she was starting to blush.

"Thank ya kindly, Gertie," he smiled as he took the basket from her hand. "This'll surely come in handy."

They stood there staring into each other's eyes until Homer groaned, "Come on Elmer, time to go!"

Elmer made a snap decision to give Gertie a kiss on the cheek and then jumped up on the wagon. A huge smile came across Gertie's face as she touched her cheek. Homer yelled at the mules and began to turn the team around. As they headed down the trail out to the main road, Gertie waved goodbye and watched until they were out of sight.

Angie could hear Homer criticizing Elmer for his behavior with Gertie, ranting and raving, accusing him of being downright ridiculous, but Elmer didn't seem to mind. The heated words went on from Homer for what seemed like an hour or more, but never a word escaped Elmer's mouth. Only a little laugh once in a while.

Late that afternoon, they arrived at the little town of Sweet Springs and found a corral next to the blacksmith shop where their mules would spend the night. After making an agreement, Homer paid the owner to allow them to park the wagon for the night.

"We'll be in Independence tomorrow," Elmer told Angie. "Then we'll be gettin' a new wagon and some supplies fore the wagon train leaves on the 15th."

Angie was beginning to like Elmer, but was still unsure of Homer. He seemed so gruff and sometimes mean.

"Where can a body get a decent meal around here?" Homer asked the blacksmith.

"At the saloon down the street," the big burly man answered. "But I don't think you'll want to take the little girl in there."

"Aw, she's alright," Homer replied as he took Angie by the arm.

Elmer removed Homer's grasp and took Angie by the hand. "Stay by me, I'll make sure you'll be alright."

Angie smiled up at him and stayed close by his side as they entered the only saloon in town. It was loud and filled with smoke. Angie held her nose, but to no avail. Her eyes were beginning to burn from all the smoke and she wished she could leave this horrible place.

"Over here," Elmer said as he guided her to a table in the corner. Homer had already gone up to the bar.

As they sat down, Elmer looked sympathetically at Angie. "Don't worry, little lady. We'll eat and then be out of here in no time."

Angie looked around her and was fascinated by the piano player. The music that came from the old instrument was fast and friendly, and the few ladies that were in the saloon were in brightly colored dresses and laughing. But mostly she saw men playing cards and enjoying a drink on this hot summer evening. She realized most of the people were staring at her, and it made her feel uncomfortable.

Where are all the families? She asked herself, *Where are the children?*

"Supper's a'comin," Homer said as he set himself a drink down on the table, and one before Elmer, and then sat down at the table to guzzle the cold beverage.

"They's got any milk in this place for the youngin'?" Elmer asked his brother.

"Didn't think to ask," Homer answered as he continued to stare at the piano player and the colorfully dressed lady that leaned against the wall listening to the music.

"Stay right here, missy," Elmer said to Angie, "I'll find ya somethin' to drink."

Angie kept her eyes on Homer who was more interested in the goings on in the saloon than in her.

"Here ya are," Elmer sat a glass of sassafras down in front of Angie. "Fraid they ain't got no milk."

"That's alright," Angie said and tasted her first glass of soda water. It tasted a bit strange but quenched her thirst.

Elmer tried to talk to Angie to distract her from the business of the saloon, and was relieved when the steaks arrived.

The owner set down a steak in front of Homer, and one in front of Elmer.

"Hey!" Elmer objected, "Got anythin' for the little lady?"

"Soups coming" the grumpy saloon owner replied as he walked away.

"Soup?" he asked as he turned to Homer.

"Steaks a little too much for a little girl, don'tcha think?" Homer answered.

"She could use the meat for the long trip ahead of us," Elmer reasoned.

"Soups good enough for her," Homer said as he shoved a huge slice of meat into his mouth.

"We're supposed to be takin' good care of her!" Elmer objected.

"We is!" Homer angrily began to seethe. His eyes became narrow and he warned Elmer with just a look.

"There's your soup," the owner said as he set the huge bowl down in front of Angie.

"An' some bread with that," Elmer told the man waiting on them.

The saloon owner looked annoyed, but came back with a couple large slices of bread and set them down in front of Angie.

"Well, eat why don't ya," Homer pointed to Angie's bowl, "Can't be wastin' it. Long way to go tomorrow an' not sure what we'll find to eat at Independence."

The soup was bland, but there were a few vegetables at the bottom of the broth. The bread was better and she ate both slices.

Elmer cut a large chunk of meat off his steak, chopped it into pieces and dumped it into Angie's bowl. She smiled up at him and gratefully accepted it. She ate the meat, vegetables and bread, and realized she was full. All that was left was broth.

"If ya ain't gonna eat all your soup, that's fine with me, but I don't wanna hear yer hungry later on, ya hear?" Homer shoved his face too close to Angie's for her own comfort.

She nodded and shoved the half empty bowl a few inches away from her.

Homer grabbed the bowl and proceeded to drink down the rest of the soup like it was a cup of water.

"Well, let's go," Elmer suggested. "We all could use a good night's sleep."

Angie was glad to be climbing under her own blanket and to be by herself. Elmer was nice to her, but she still didn't feel safe around Homer. As her eyes started to get heavy, she could hear Homer and Elmer talking to each other about reaching Independence the next day to meet up with the wagon train. She heard them setting up their tents, and that was all she remembered.

Another early morning came for Angie. She began to realize it would be just the start of many early mornings. After a plate of flapjacks, some bacon, as well as some coffee for Homer and Elmer, Angie waved goodbye to the piano player who blew her a kiss. One of the ladies in the saloon giggled at the little girl and the three started the last leg of their journey to Independence, Missouri.

The skies were threatening and the rain began to gently fall, causing the road to turn to mud. Homer was not pleased at this turn of events and made his distress known. Angie sat back against the side of the wagon and placed the Bible on her lap. She enjoyed trying to pick out words she recognized and it helped pass the time. Once in a while she would look up and gaze out the back at the three mules tied to the back of the wagon. She decided to name them, Franklin, Washington and Hamilton. The two mules in the front would be named Betsy and Martha. She didn't know if the mules were males or females, but she didn't seem to care either.

The skies soon began to clear and the sun brought out the warmth. Angie found herself leaning out the back, resting her chin on her arms, talking to the mules. The animals seemed to understand her with their sympathetic eyes.

Soon, Angie noticed several other wagons following behind them and she no longer felt alone. She was interested in seeing new faces and wondered if they were headed to Independence as well. A little girl was sitting next to her father in front of the wagon behind them. She waved to Angie and Angie timidly waved back. More and more wagons sat along the side of the road and Angie realized they were finally entering the bustling town of Independence. The wagon finally stopped and Homer tied up the mules in front of a General Store and then disappeared down the street on foot.

Angie was anxious to get out of the wagon and stretch her legs, but Elmer instructed her to stay in the wagon while he walked around the wagon and checked the mules. After what seemed like an eternity, Homer came out of the store and talked with Elmer about the provisions he had arranged; a new pioneer schooner especially built for the one way journey, pulled by four mules instead of two, tying the fifth mule to the back for an alternate, as well as two to three months of food, soap, cooking utensils and tools. Elmer lifted Angie out of the back of the wagon and she walked with them to a small dinner house where they could freshen up and eat a hearty meal of stew and bread. After the meal, Angie walked with Elmer back to the wagon to wait for Homer to bring the larger wagon. She became excited when she saw the new prairie schooner coming down the road with Homer sitting next to the previous owner. The fresh white canvas stretched over the hooped framework looked welcoming and more spacious.

After taking his horses off the prairie schooner and hooking them up to the old ragged wagon that had once belonged to Homer and Elmer, the jolly heavy man with the huge mustache waved goodbye to Homer, yelled "Git Up!" to his horses, and pulled the wagon away to sell to someone else.

While Homer was hitching four of the mules to the front of the wagon, Elmer was busy finishing loading their belongings inside the wagon from where he had left them next to the boardwalk. Angie helped hand the lighter items up to him. She was anxious to climb up and see what the new wagon looked like inside.

Homer went into the General Store and had the clerk help him bring out wooden crates, barrels and sacks of flour, beans, dried fruit and vegetables, slabs of smoked bacon packed in bran, jerky, coffee, sugar and lard. He also bought eggs packed in cornmeal, salt and pepper, and some baking powder. Among the other items he bought were a shovel, broad axe, and a mallet. He already had his hunting knife, shotgun and pistol, so the only other essentials he needed was horseshoes for the mules and a change of clothes.

Elmer took Angie by the hand and led her into the store and looked around until he found just what was on his mind.

"There ya be," Elmer said as he reached up and took down a pretty white sunbonnet. He placed it on Angie's head and tied it haphazardly under her chin, "For the sun."

A smile spread across Angie's face and she hugged him around his waist.

"Yer welcome, little lady," Elmer smiled.

"Quit wastin' our money!" Homer scolded Elmer as he came back into the store.

Elmer ignored him and placed the $2.00 on the counter.

"Last time I give you any money," Homer fumed as he grabbed a bag of chewing tobacco and a new felt hat for himself.

The down mattress that the McKennas had provided was placed on top of the boxes of supplies, leveled out to make a bed for Angie. She climbed inside and marveled at the fresh smell of seasoned hardwood and the cleanliness of the fresh new canvas that hovered over her.

Before the sun set that night, Homer drove the wagon up to a camp located just a short distance from the old Independence Landing situated north of the city of Independence. This would be the point from where the wagon train would gather and start out the very next day for the West.

Angie thought she would be excited about finally starting the trip to her aunt and uncle's home and within two to three months be able to settle into her new life, but she wasn't.

As Elmer volunteered to take care of the mules, Homer set up the tents next to the wagon.

"Good night, little lady," Elmer called inside the wagon.

"Good night, Elmer," Angie answered as she lay down on the feathered mattress and wrapped her blanket around her. Panic began to fill her heart.

Tomorrow we're actually leaving for California, she thought, *a long way from everything I know. A long way from everyone I know. A long way from Columbia, Missouri, from Elma and George, from Pastor Johnson and Miss O'Brien.*

And then she smiled, *And a long way from Pearl!*

****

CHAPTER SIX

The Trail

After lining up at Independence Landing, wagons sat waiting for others to arrive and travelers spent the time checking supplies and livestock.

Angie watched as the men began to leave their wagons and all head in one direction. A young man ran up to their wagon and said, "The wagon master wants the head of the wagon household up in the front, now!"

Homer grumbled to Elmer, "You wait here, I'll go see what he wants."

As Angie watched him walk away, her curiosity got the best of her. She slipped out of the wagon and followed him about 10 paces behind. As they got closer to the crowd of men, she stood slightly behind Homer.

Everyone was talking among themselves when finally a middle aged man with a booming voice spoke up.

"I'm here your wagon master. My name is Bishop Taylor. From this point on, I'm the law on this trail. I have nearly 40 wagons I'm responsible for and the only way I'm gonna get the majority of you to California is if you do what I say, when I say it, and exactly how I say it. Do I make myself clear?"

Some muttering went on among the men, but a unanimous agreement could be heard.

"The wagons being pulled by horses and mules will be leaving today," Wagon Master Taylor shouted. "Horses and mules need greener grass to eat to survive. The wagons being pulled by oxen will leave in a couple days with Wagon Master Billings. The oxen can survive on scrub grass and what's left by the horses and mules."

Angie peered forward so she could get a better glimpse of Wagon Master Taylor, when she caught Homer's attention out of the corner of his eye.

"What in tarnation are you doin' here?!" he glared at Angie, "I oughta tan yer hide! Now get back to the wagon!"

Angie immediately turned and ran the entire distance until she reached their spot in line.

"Where have ya been?!" Elmer yelled at Angie as soon as he spotted her. "Ya had me darn near feared to death! Don't ya ever go wanderin' off agin, ya hear?"

Angie nodded her head and quickly climbed in the back of the wagon, afraid of what Homer might do when he returned.

Elmer came to the back of the wagon and continued his lecture, "It's gonna be way too dangerous out there. Stay close!"

"I will," Angie said as she grabbed her blanket and held it close to her.

"Ya better or you'll be dead for sure!" Elmer gave her a serious look.

"From here on, everybody walks," Homer said when he came back to the wagon. "The wagon master says we gotta take it easy on the horses and mules. They's gotta lot a weight to pull all the way to California."

"But she's just a little girl!" Elmer objected, "She can't walk all the way to California!"

"She walks!" Homer argued.

"That's alright," Angie said as she climbed out of the wagon, "I don't mind walking. I like to walk."

"Who'll be steering the mules?" Elmer asked.

"We lead 'em," Homer replied, "Let's get ready! The wagon train will be leavin' soon."

Several hours had worn on, and the wagon train was finally beginning to move. That first day on the trail, Angie found it was going to be much harder than she could ever imagine. She was walking beside Elmer when Homer turned to them and said,

"We all gotta share in the work, and that means you too, little girl!"

Angie mustered up her courage and said to Homer, "But my aunt paid you to take care of me and you're supposed to do the work, not me."

"Listen to me you spoiled little weasel," Homer exploded, "I ain't paid to do all the work myself, I'm paid to get ya to your aunt's house and that's all! We all do our part, ya hear me?!"

"She hears ya!" Elmer barked back at his brother. He turned to Angie and said, "Don't worry, I'll help ya."

Angie didn't say a word; she just kept her eyes on the ground. Homer frightened her to her very core and she always tried to keep her distance from him.

Late that afternoon, the wagon master designated the place where the travelers would spend the night and directed the wagon train to form a circle in order to pen in the livestock. Campfires were started and women began preparing the evening meal.

"Go get some firewood," Homer ordered Angie. "Gotta get us a fire started." Elmer brought out some food to prepare. Angie looked around her and found that people had already picked up most of the excess wood lying around. She scurried around the wagon and found a couple pieces and brought them to where Homer was digging a hole for the campfire.

"That ain't gonna get us through the night," Homer scowled. "Go find some more."

Angie wandered around looking for more, but whenever she spotted a branch or piece of wood, someone else always beat her to it. Tears started to come to her eyes from sheer frustration. She was afraid that Homer would yell at her again.

She noticed a couple boys with their arms loaded with wood coming out of the woods.

"Can you show me where you found that?" Angie asked them.

"Just give her some" the older boy said to the younger one, "We got plenty."

She was so grateful to the boys and kept thanking them over and over again. She then immediately ran back to the campsite with a couple good-size pieces of wood and set them down proudly in front of Homer. He didn't bother to look up. He just reached out and grabbed the wood to throw on the fire.

"Come help me with the supper," Elmer said to Angie, hoping to divert Homer from asking Angie to go collect more wood. He didn't feel it was safe for Angie to go any farther away from their camp.

After they cleaned up from their meal, Homer sat by the fire, stirring the ashes with a stick and chewing on a mouthful of tobacco. Angie looked around at the reflection of the campfires against the dark evening sky. Voices were echoing against the night and someone was singing. She glanced around at the wagons that were settled in for the night when she saw someone staring at her. It was a girl from the camp next to theirs. Angie looked away, but every time she looked back, the girl was still staring at her. It made Angie feel uncomfortable and she asked if she could go to bed early. Homer waved her goodbye and Elmer got up to make sure she got into the wagon alright.

"Do you think he'll ever like me?" Angie asked Elmer about Homer.

"Oh, he likes you alright," Elmer told her, "He's just not used to females. Now shut yer eyes an' don't worry about nothin'."

The bugle went off early the next morning. She woke with a start, and immediately sat up. Realizing it was the wakeup call for the camp, she yawned and stretched. Homer was already calling Angie to make breakfast. As she climbed out of the wagon, Homer and Elmer were packing up their pup tents that served as their shelter.

Elmer was there beside her, teaching her how to make coffee and flatbread. Angie sipped on her first cup of coffee and made faces, reflecting on how awful it tasted to her.

"You'd better get used to it," Elmer told her. "The water's not always safe and a lot of it tastes bad. The coffee will help it taste better."

Angie couldn't imagine how anything could taste any worse.

After the mules were hitched to the wagon and the wagon train began to move along the trail, Angie found herself walking beside the wagon by herself, daydreaming about her new home. She imagined it would be a big house, with flowers in the yard and maybe a creek where she could play. She hoped her aunt and uncle had a dog or cat she could have for her own, and maybe a swing hung from a tree.

Angie could see the girl from the wagon up ahead stop in the middle of her tracks and wait for Angie's wagon to catch up. She then walked beside Angie and said "Hi, my name's Mahhhhgaret and I'm 13 years old. What's your name?"

"Angie Owens," Angie looked at her with curiosity, "and I'm 11 years old."

"You sure enough look small for your age," Margaret smiled.

"I'm not small for my age," Angie objected. "And you're big for your age!"

"I'm not trying to hurt your feelings," Margaret stuttered. "And I guess I am a bit tall for 13."

Angie didn't respond.

"Those your family?" Margaret asked as she pointed at Homer and Elmer.

"No, my family's dead," Angie answered, "I'm going to California to live with my aunt and uncle."

"They're not really my family either," Margaret said as she nodded toward the wagon up ahead, "They say they are, but I know the real truth."

"What truth?" Angie looked up at the tall girl with the soft brown braids.

"I'm really a princess," Margaret confided. "My real name is Margaret, Princess of London, England, and I was stolen by pirates when I was a tiny baby. They brought me across the ocean to this country and sold me to these people I'm with. They spent all their money to get me. That's how bad they wanted a baby."

"How do you know you're a princess?" Angie asked skeptically.

"I have a birthmark, right here on my arm." She showed Angie a small mole. "It says that I am a princess. Only royalty has birthmarks. Everything else I figured out on my own."

Angie thought about what Margaret said for a few minutes and then asked her, "Why are you going to California?"

"Because they're taking me as far away as they can," Margaret answered. "You see, the Prince of Spain is coming to rescue me and take me back to England so he can marry me."

"Oh," was all Angie said, still skeptical of Margaret's story.

"You see, he's coming on a winged horse…" Margaret started.

"A what?!" Angie stopped her.

"A winged horse!" she responded, "Haven't you ever heard of a winged horse?"

Angie shook her head.

"Well, they're very beautiful, all white with a very long mane and tail, and they have feathered wings coming out of their backs so they can fly," Margaret was excited to explain.

"They can fly?" Angie's eyes got big.

"Of course they can," Margaret smiled, "That's why they have wings!"

"I wish I had wings," Angie told her, "Then I could fly all the way to California. My feet are beginning to hurt."

"Mine too," Margaret agreed, "New boots are hard to walk in."

"I think I have a blister," Angie confided in Margaret, "but I don't want to tell Homer. He'll just yell at me, Maybe I'll tell Elmer."

"They're really not your family?" Margaret looked surprised.

"No, they're just hired to get me across the country," Angie told her, "so I can live with my aunt and uncle in Sacramento."

"Wow," Margaret said. "They must be rich if they can hire someone to take you all the way to Sacramento."

"I don't know about that,' Angie said as she watched her feet walk the ground in front of her.

"They could be a duke or duchess or something like that and they just haven't told you yet," Margaret suggested.

Angie only laughed to herself and said, "I don't think so."

"But they gotta be rich!" Margaret insisted, "You wait! You'll see!"

That night sitting around the campfire, Angie whispered in Elmer's ear, "Elmer, I think I have a blister on my foot. It hurts something awful."

"Let me see your foot, little lady," Elmer said as he held out his hand.

She carefully stretched out her leg and Elmer slowly removed her boot and stocking and examined the bottom of her foot.

"Yep, sure 'nough," Elmer said as he pointed to Angie's heel, "There's one right there!"

He turned to Homer. "She needs to ride in the wagon tomorrow."

"Everybody walks," Homer responded.

"Now that just ain't gonna happen!" Elmer protested, "We here supposed to be takin' real good care of her and she needs to let this thing heal!"

Homer was silent for a minute and then relented, "Just tomorrow then. Don't wanna strain the mules."

"Oh, for land's sake!" Elmer reacted, "She's just a tiny little thing. Don't weight more than a pup."

Elmer found some salve to soothe Angie's foot and Angie rubbed it over her heel. He then picked up Angie and carried her to the back of the wagon where she climbed inside.

"Elmer," Angie said, "is there such a thing as a winged horse?"

"I hear some books says there is," Elmer responded, "but me, why I never did see one. Why? Where'd you hear about a winged horse?"

"Margaret told me," Angie answered.

"Oh, made a new friend did ya?" Elmer smiled. "Well, friends is good. An' imaginations is good too. The more ya got of both, the better off ya are, little lady. Now get to sleep and dream about winged horses, ya hear?"

The days started to run into each other. Angie's foot was much better and she began walking most of the distance each day. Her boots began to form to her feet and become more comfortable. Margaret was her faithful companion full of interesting stories, most of them from her imagination, but she helped the day pass and was someone Angie could relate to, making up stories from her own fantasies. When their stories became too outlandish, they would both look at each other and burst out laughing.

Besides storytelling, the girls grabbed pieces of wood that others missed and tossed them onto the tarps that hung under the wagons. Margaret would help Angie fill her tarp and Angie helped Margaret fill her tarp in return. If they couldn't find any wood, they would collect buffalo chips and pretend that they were collecting huge nuggets of gold to avoid the realization of what they were really handling.

"By the end of this day, we'll be rich!" Margaret declared.

"Look how much gold I have in my tarp!" Angie agreed.

"We'll be able to buy our own castle and have servants and sleep in grand beds with silk covers and wear fancy gowns!" Margaret added.

"And go to fancy Balls with handsome princes and everyone will want to dance with us!" Angie laughed.

"And marry us!" Margaret squealed.

Their fairy tales always brought Angie and Margaret many hours of happiness.

Suddenly, they heard a scream from behind them. They turned to see people running to one of the back wagons on the trail. Margaret and Angie ran to join the others, curious to see what had happened. As they neared the wagon, they heard more screaming and crying.

As they peered in between the crowd, they saw a little girl lying on the ground, motionless.

"She fell out of the back of the wagon!" someone said to another.

"Is she dead?" Angie asked Margaret.

"I don't know," Margaret responded.

The little girl's mother was sobbing as her husband was trying to get a response from his daughter.

"Get back to the wagon!" Angie heard Homer's voice behind her. She immediately turned and began walking back where Elmer was standing, holding the reins to the mules. Margaret was with her.

"What's goin' on?" Elmer asked her.

"A little girl fell out of a wagon!" Margaret was eager to tell him.

"Is she alright?" Elmer asked the girls.

The girls shrugged their shoulders and waited for Homer to come back.

After a short while, Wagon Master Taylor rode by them on his horse, heading back to the front of the wagon train. He looked grim and yelled, "Everyone, get ready to move on!"

Homer arrived soon after that.

"Is the little girl alright?" Elmer asked him.

"She's dead," Homer answered, "Her parents are staying behind to bury her. They'll wait and join the oxen wagon train when they catch up to 'em."

Angie and Margaret stood silent for a moment, trying to absorb the news.

"She's dead!" Margaret whispered to Angie.

"I know," Angie said, "I feel bad for their family. I know how they feel. It really hurts."

"I never saw anybody dead before," Margaret confided, "Have you?"

"I don't want to talk about this anymore," Angie told her and started walking with the onset of the wagon train, resuming the journey.

Around the campfires that evening, the death of the little girl was the main topic everywhere. Angie was beginning to get sick to her stomach, just thinking about it, and covered her ears. Homer droned on and on about others he heard of dying on the wagon train trails over the past years.

She rose and said, "I'm going to bed now."

"Go, go!" Homer waved her away.

"See ya in the morning, little lady," Elmer smiled to her.

As she covered herself with her blanket and sunk down into the mattress, she could feel tears starting to run down her cheeks.

Stop it! She angrily chided herself, *Crying won't change anything! People live, people die. It just happens that way.* After a few minutes of containing her emotions, she stared out the back of the wagon at the light from the campfires, the stars in the sky, and the moon that was in its full glory.

Dear God, she prayed, *if I die tonight, help me not to be afraid. I miss my momma and daddy and Billy. Please take good care of them until I get there and then I'll help you. I know it's hard to take care of so many people. Get lots of rest and I'll talk to you tomorrow. Good night God. Love, Angie Owens. Amen.*

****

CHAPTER SEVEN
The Fort

The first month passed with the telling of many more fantasy stories between Angie and Margaret, which became a pleasant distraction from the more than half a dozen deaths that had occurred. Most of the accidents were due to falling under heavy-laden wagons, rattlesnake bites, and one childbirth death. Even though grief ran through the wagon train, the growing death toll became less and less shocking and more and more common.

The wagon train was making good time. The trail was well worn from the thousands of pioneers who had made the trek in the past 13 years before them. What used to take five months to cross the nation, could now be walked in 2 to 3 months, if the weather was good. New, easier trails had been found and ferries had been built across rivers. It was important to cross the mountains before the snows fell, and everyone was pushing hard because of their late start. This would be the last wagon train crossing the mountains this year. Along with the fast pace and poor feeding conditions, the trip was beginning to take a toll on the horses and mules. The plan was to reach Fort Laramie as quickly as they could so that they could get fresh replacements.

The Blanket of Blessings 123

At Fort Laramie, horse traders would buy the spent animals and sell healthy animals in their place. The horses and mules would then be properly fed and rested until they were returned to good condition, and then sold to the next wagon train to come through their area. Oxen could usually make the trip across country without needing to be traded out, but were a lot slower in making the journey.

Angie looked up at the sky and was bothered by how dark it was growing for mid-afternoon. The air felt unusually warm and the winds were picking up speed.

"A storm is coming," Margaret told her.

"We need to keep movin'," Homer instructed. "Gotta find shelter."

Soon Wagon Master Taylor directed the wagon train away from the main trail and over closer to the base of the rolling hills.

"Circle up and hunker down!" he instructed, "Tie your livestock to your wagons. Tie down your belongings and get inside or under your wagons!"

The travelers hurried to get themselves situated and Elmer lifted Angie up into the wagon.

"Stay there," Elmer instructed as he left to help Homer.

Angie crawled under her blanket and could feel the hot wind coming through the back of the wagon. The wind was getting blustery and the temperatures were uncomfortable. It was but a few moments when the rain began to fall and soon became a heavy torrent. The muddy water drove Homer and Elmer out from under the wagon and they climbed inside to keep dry. Homer covered the openings with tarps to keep the rain out. It was crowded, and with the three of them huddled together, the air inside the wagon felt humid and stifling.

"Don't have time for all this rain," Homer complained, "We're losin' time. I'm tired of this wagon train. It's takin' way too long to get there. I shoulda never hired on for this job."

"Here," Elmer said handing Homer a piece of jerky, "have somethin' to eat." And then he gave Angie a piece to chew on.

"I'm not just jawin', "Homer said to Elmer. There's gotta be a faster way to get to Sacramento. I'm running outta patience with only twenty miles a day. We can make it faster on our own."

"I don't think that's safe," Elmer told him.

"Safe?!" Homer remarked, "People's dying all round us every day!"

The wind began to blow harder than before, shaking the wagon violently. Angie felt fear flow through her, praying that the wagon wouldn't tip over.

Elmer wanted to change the subject. "Angie, ya ever heard the song 'Sweet Molly McQueen'?"

Angie shook her head 'no'.

"It goes somethin like this…," Elmer smiled and then sang Angie a silly song that made her laugh.

"Teach me the song," Angie begged.

Elmer and Angie spent the next hour singing and changing the words to the song which made the tune even sillier.

"That's 'nough!" Homer exploded. "Can't take no more!"

The silence was sudden, and only the sound of rain and wind could be heard.

"Best take a nap," Elmer whispered in Angie's ear. "Not much else to do 'til this storm passes."

Angie laid her head against Elmer's arm and closed her eyes.

The storm stayed through the night, and by early morning, the muddy roads made it difficult to get started.

When Elmer saw Angie struggling to walk through the mud as the wagon train began to move, he trudged over and picked her up, placing her up on top of the mule that was trailing in the back.

Homer went to say something, but Elmer cut him off, "She's riding! Don't want to hear a word about it!"

Homer glared at Elmer. "You're forgettin' yerself Elmer! I'll square with you later!"

Elmer ignored him and went back up to the front to help pull the tired mules through the mud.

The further the wagon train moved, the more Homer complained. The roads were beginning to dry out, but the mud was caked on the mule's feet and wagon wheels. After they stopped for the night, Homer sat chipping the dried mud from the mule's hoofs, swearing under his breath and cursing his decision to take on the journey. "No money's worth this much sweat and blood."

"Wagon Master Taylor says we'll be in Fort Laramie tomorrow." As Elmer worked on the wagon wheels, he tried to encourage Homer, "We can get a warm bath and a hot steak there. An' some fresh mules."

Homer just grunted and Angie knew better than to get in his way.

****

The wagon train was only a few hours from Fort Laramie and Angie could hear cheers in the air when the settlement appeared in sight.

As they entered town, Angie had her first sighting of American Indians as she walked beside Elmer. Many of the Plains Indians had come to Fort Laramie to trade and work for food. Angie was fascinated with their tanned skin and long jet black hair.

"Be careful of them savages," Homer told Angie. "They'll eat ya for supper!"

Angie stepped in behind Elmer, peering out at the people with the different clothes and different features.

"Aw," Elmer laughed, "they won't eat ya! These here Injuns are peaceful."

Angie trusted Elmer and felt a little relieved but kept her distance just in case.

"You'll have the day to get your business done," Wagon Master Taylor instructed, "Best to get fresh horses and mules, and stock up on food and water if needed. Between here and Fort Casper, the water is drinkable, but tastes bad. We'll be heading for the mountains, so make sure you get rid of your excess weight. Dump everything you don't need. It'll make it easier getting over the passes."

Homer and Elmer consolidated the food and dumped some wooden crates and barrels. Then they untied the mules and walked them to the horse traders down the road who were waiting to make money on the pioneers. They allowed Angie to go with them and Elmer showed her how to lead one of the mules. It made her feel important to be leading her own animal. She hoped everyone noticed her, especially Margaret.

Unexpectedly, they heard a horse and rider coming up fast behind them. As it sped by, it startled the mules and Elmer helped Angie keep control of the mule she was leading as it began to rear up. They watched the rider press on down the road until he was out of sight.

"Ya darn fool!" Elmer yelled after the hasty horseman and then turned to Angie as he got the mule settled down. "You alright, little lady?"

"Aw, quit babyin' her!" Homer told him, "Ya can see she's alright, can't ya?"

"I'm alright," Angie assured Elmer, "just a little scared."

"Some people just ain't got the good sense God gave 'em," Elmer said looking down the road at the dust that was left behind, "Coulda got somebody killed".

"Yeah, well, nobody's dead, so let's get these mules traded in for some fresh ones and get back to the wagon," Homer suggested, "I'm thinkin' 'bout that steak we was talkin' 'bout earlier."

"It's not even noon," Elmer protested.

"Lunch, supper, it all tastes the same," Homer smiled.

Angie had to admit she hadn't seen Homer smile since they left Gertie's house. She thought he actually had a nice smile under his grubby appearance.

As they returned to the wagon with the five mules that Homer had just purchased, one of the men from the wagon train ran by yelling for everyone to come to the main square for a meeting. "Come now! Come now!" he yelled.

The Blanket of Blessings 129

"What now?!" Homer grumbled to himself. After Elmer helped him tie up the mules to the wagon, they began walking down the road. Angie held Elmer's hand as Margaret ran up and began walking next to her.

"I've been looking all over for you," Margaret said, "I couldn't find you anywhere!"

"I went to help take the mules to the trader. We got new ones!" Angie explained.

"What do you think Mr. Taylor has to say?" Margaret asked.

"Don't know," Angie responded, "but it sounds important."

More and more people from the wagon train began to join the parade down the road until they finally gathered at the square. After a few minutes, Wagon Master Taylor stood in the middle of the square and made the following announcement:

"Listen up! A messenger arrived today to let us know that Wagon Master Billings' group was hit directly by a late season tornado a couple of days ago. This is not common here. They usually hit in the spring and summer, if they do. A lot of people were killed and even more injured. Most lost their wagons and everything they owned.

I am going to ask you to do something that may seem unreasonable, but it would be the kind of thing that would show what kind of people you are. We need people to turn back with their wagons and help bring the survivors back here to Fort

Laramie. I'm even asking some of you to allow these people to ride with you all the way to California if need be.

Everything they had is gone, maybe even family. They need your help. We can't just leave 'em out there to die. Colonel Wilson has offered a group of his soldiers to go with you and help bury the dead and bring the survivors back to the fort. You will then move on to Sacramento with Wagon Master Billings and those that are healthy enough to travel. The rest of us will move on tomorrow as scheduled. Do I have any volunteers?"

Everyone searched each other's faces, and the crowd was silent.

"Do I have any volunteers?" Wagon Master Taylor repeated his question.

The crowd remained silent.

"Alright," their leader said regrettably. "If anyone changes their mind, the soldiers will be leaving in the morning. You have until then to decide. You can go with them, or come with me. Nothing further will be said."

That afternoon, the soldiers loaded a wagon with supplies. Many of the travelers donated food and water in hopes of relieving some of their guilt for not going back to help the other wagon train.

Elmer felt sad for the people who had weathered the tornado and survived, but also knew that Homer was bent on moving on as quickly as possible.

After a full stomach and a mouth full of chewing tobacco, Homer decided to walk the town and spend some time in a saloon. Angie and Margaret sat by Margaret's wagon and played with one of Margaret's dolls.

"Maggie," Margaret's mother said, "don't you think you're getting a might old for dolls?"

"No, mom," Margaret answered, "I love my dolls."

Her mother laughed and shook her head as she went back to straightening their wagon.

"Maggie?" Angie said, "Why'd she call you Maggie?"

"I think they call me that so no one will know who I really am. If they call me Margaret, people will figure out I am Princess Margaret," she answered.

Angie smiled and went back to combing the doll's hair.

"You know someday we'll have real babies," Margaret said, "not just dolls."

"Not me," Angie told her. "Not ever going to get married."

"Not even to a prince?" Margaret asked.

"Nope," Angie shook her head.

"Well, I am!" Margaret smiled. "You'll see."

Elmer sat at their own wagon, keeping an eye on the girls a distance away. He felt the responsibility to make sure Angie arrived safely to her aunt's home, no matter how Homer felt.

After Margaret was instructed to help with supper, Angie began to wander back to her wagon.

Two Indian boys caught her attention, playing a kind of game with rocks and sticks in the road. She watched them, trying to figure out the rules of the game when one of the boys noticed her. He stopped playing and just stared at her, and then whispered to his friend. Angie became nervous and turned to continue her walk back to her wagon. The boy walked over to her and stopped in front of her. Angie and the boy just stared at each other, neither one moving. Suddenly, the boy reached out and touched her hair. At first, Angie started to panic, but then realized he meant her no harm. She understood that her blonde hair was probably a rare sight in this part of the country and he was just curious. She smiled at him, and then he smiled back and turned to run back to his friend and continue their game.

The encounter gave Angie a funny feeling, one that she had not felt before, somewhat uncomfortable, but yet, somehow familiar. She had never been that close to someone of a different culture before and she wasn't sure how to react. The feeling stayed with her as she returned to the wagon.

As she lay in bed that night, Angie thought about the Indian boy, and then about Margaret's words.

Am I going to get married someday? She asked herself. *How silly! Margaret talks about things I don't even care about. The whole idea makes my stomach sick. I don't want no boy telling me what to do. Nobody like Homer yelling at me. I think I'll be happier just by myself. Nope, not going to get married! Ever!*

****

CHAPTER EIGHT

The Crossing

By morning, three wagons had decided to turn back to help the stranded survivors of the other wagon train. Everyone else, including Homer, Elmer and Angie pressed on toward Platte Bridge Station.

The wagon train followed the North Platte River and found that the grass was mostly gone due to wagon trains that had come through during the spring and summer months, leaving very little for the late wagon trains. The horses and mules were struggling to find enough to eat. Two more accidental deaths and one suicide along the way was reported and the Rocky Mountains loomed ahead of them. As they neared the mountain range, the days were slowly getting colder, encouraging the pioneers to press on as quickly as they could, but not quick enough for Homer. As the days ran from one into the other, Homer was getting more and more impatient with the slow but steady pace. Every day he talked to Elmer about leaving the wagon train and going on by themselves, but so far, Elmer had been able to dissuade him.

The Blanket of Blessings

Finally arriving at Platte Bridge Station, the wagon train had dwindled from the original 40 wagons down to 29. Before them lay the treacherous North Platte River which had to be crossed. In the past, hundreds of emigrants had drowned trying to cross the rivers that lay in Wyoming. In an attempt to make crossing the river easier, ferries had been established by Mormons who named the crossing Mormon Ferry Post.

As the wagon train came to a stop, arrangements were being made between Wagon Master Taylor and the ferry master.

Wagon Master Taylor rounded his group together. "We'll begin crossing right away. The water is high for this time of year, and the crossing will be slow. Could be up to an hour for the ferry to get across and back. That means it could take 3 days to get everyone across. Everyone is to wait on the other side until the entire wagon train has crossed. The ferry master says all Mormons can cross at no cost, everyone else will be charged $3.00 per wagon and 50 cents per person."

"I ain't Mormon! What if I don't wanna pay?" someone yelled out.

"What if I can't afford to pay?" someone else hollered, "I spent all my money on fresh horses in Laramie."

"The only other place to cross," the wagon master answered, "is downstream at the South Platte River. You're welcome to go the extra miles downstream and meet up with us on the other side, but be forewarned, the South Platte River is a swamp. You'll be facing a much harder crossing with mud, insects and disease. The choice is yours."

The people muttered among themselves and eventually lined up to make the crossing. Only one wagon refused to pay the fee and decided to attempt the swamp.

"We'll see you on the other side!" they yelled as they waved goodbye to the train.

The Smith wagon was toward the rear of the line and Homer was not pleased with his position. He left their camp to have a talk with Mr. Bishop Taylor.

"What's say you move us up to the front," Homer said to Bishop with a smile on his face, "I kin make it worth yer while. Got some extra money here." With that he patted his pocket.

"You're the fifth person to try to bribe me," Bishop responded, "Sorry. You'll be crossing tomorrow if you're lucky. The next day more likely."

The smile quickly left Homer's face and a scowl replaced it. "I can't wait that long," Homer exploded, "I got a time schedule to meet. I gotta get this here wagon to Sacramento soon as possible."

"Like I told the others, you either wait on this side of the river, or that side," Bishop told him and began to walk away, "We'll all be leaving together."

"We'll see 'bout that!" Homer yelled after him.

Elmer spent the rest of the day trying to reason with Homer while Angie sat by the river with Margaret and watched the ferry painstakingly take one wagon with their family and livestock across at a time. Several families had more livestock than could cross at one time, and had to make several crossings.

One set of mules started to panic from the movement of the water under them and they reared up on the ferry, which was no more than wooden planks tied together and nailed down to floating logs. The owner tried to settle them back down, but to no avail. The riders began to panic, yelling for help as the raft began rocking back and forth until the mules broke through the flimsy railing and fell over the side, taking the wagon with it. One man fell in the river with them, but was pulled back onboard the ferry, drenched and cold. Fear ran through the remainder of the emigrants who were waiting to cross, as they watched the wagon and mules being swept downstream. The ferry master was able to assure them that they'd be alright, and how to handle the horses and mules so there'd be no more accidents.

It took a while for the railing to be repaired, which was pushing Homer's impatience to the breaking point. Soon the ferry resumed taking the wagons across as smoothly as before the incident. But it was not easing Homer's temper. He stomped away from their wagon and disappeared among the waiting crowd.

After a couple hours, Angie could see the worried look that was plastered on Elmer's face.

"Do you think he's alright?" she asked Elmer.

"I suppose so," he muttered while he gazed at the ground.

"Should we go look for him?" Angie asked.

"Yeah, let's go," Elmer said as he started to walk in the same direction Homer had gone. Angie trailed close behind him. They searched each wagon site until they finally found Homer, sitting with three other men in front of a small table, drinking whiskey and playing cards.

"Let's go back to the wagon," Elmer told Angie.

"But what about Homer?" she asked him.

"He's alright," Elmer assured her. "He'll come back when he's ready. Someone's gotta keep movin' the wagon up. We gotta get back there."

The ferry stopped the crossings as the sun began to sink. Campfires soon lit up the evening and supper was being prepared on both sides of the river.

Angie had been asleep for several hours when she woke to hear Homer singing as he came back to their camp. He was off-key, and slurring his words and she heard him stumbling around, trying to find his tent. After a few minutes of talking to himself, all was quiet again and Angie fell back asleep.

****

It was another long day, waiting to move up to the front of the line. Homer was in a foul mood with a bad headache and grumbling about all the money he lost at the poker game.

Elmer was frustrated that there wasn't much money left for the rest of their journey and let Homer know how he felt.

"What ya got yerself in such a snit for anyway?" Homer snapped back at Elmer, "We get more when we deliver the girl."

"We'd had more if ya hadn't lost it last night!" Elmer was upset. "Just throwing it away like it was unwanted trash! An' ya call me the fool!"

"Get away from me!" Homer screamed back, holding his head, "Can't ya see I'm in no mood to be yelled at?! My head is breakin' wide open."

"Maybe ya better think about that next time ya decide to go being stupid!" Elmer returned the yelling.

Elmer kept the wagon moving up until they reached the edge of the river. The ferry crossing was built, owned and run by the Mormon settlers who came to this part of the country years before. The ferry master asked Homer, "Be ye Mormon brother?"

"I ain't no Mormon," Homer answered, "no Jew, no Christian, an' no brother of yorn!"

"Then thy wage shall be $3.00 per wagon, and 50 cents per person," the ferry master said as he held out an open hand.

"You're nothin' but a rotten thief," Homer snarled at him.

"I'm providing a service, take it or leave it," he responded to Homer's accusation.

Homer put the money in the ferry master's hand and glared at him, "You're no better than a snake in a shallow pit."

"I'd be more careful choosing my words, brother," the ferry master said to Homer, "or you you'll be paying for your mules as well."

Homer shut his mouth, grabbed the reins and began pulling the mules toward the ferry. One of the front mules began to resist stepping onto the raft. He smacked the mule on the rear haunches and began to curse. The mule reared up and pulled back.

The ferry master tried to reason with him, but Homer wouldn't listen.

"He cannot cross," the ferry master said turning to Elmer, holding out his hand to return their money. "You will all wind up going into the river."

Elmer ignored the money, turned to Homer and grabbed the reins from his hands.

"What do ya think you're doin'?!" Homer yelled at Elmer.

"Gettin' us across this river!" Elmer planted his face directly into Homer's. "Get in the wagon and shut up! I'm takin' the mules from here!"

Homer was fuming and said under his breath, "Elmer Smith, you will live to regret this!"

"Maybe so," Elmer answered his brother,"but for now, ya need to get inta that wagon and shut yer trap!"

Homer glared at Elmer and then climbed into the wagon and began throwing things around inside.

Elmer waited for silence inside the wagon and then coaxed the mules onboard the ferry. Then he said to Angie, "Come on little lady. We'll be just fine."

She stepped onto the raft and the ferry master was right behind her.

"Hang on to the railing, miss," the ferry master told her as he pushed off the shore with his long pole.

The raft rocked gently back and forth and Elmer continued to talk soothingly to the mules. Their eyes were wide with fear, but they remained standing in their place. The wagon was chocked so that it wouldn't move, and Angie looked at the shore that was getting farther behind them, and then she saw Margaret on the shore ahead of them. She was waving at her. Angie tried to wave, but then grabbed the railing again, trying to keep her balance.

The crossing was slow but steady, and the raft finally butted itself against the other side of the river. Elmer was quick to bring the mules and wagon off, while the ferry master helped Angie step onto the muddy shoreline.

Margaret ran up to her and hugged her, "I was so scared. Were you?"

Angie nodded her head, and the girls stood aside as Elmer found a place to settle for the night.

Elmer was afraid to look inside the wagon, for fear of what Homer might say or do, so instead, he went about caring for the mules.

The girls went to the back of the wagon and Angie called to Homer, "Are you alright, Homer?"

There was no answer.

She climbed up to look inside and found everything in disarray with Homer chewing on his tobacco. She then saw her crocheted blanket wadded underneath him. She was afraid he would get his muddy boots on her blanket, or worse, his tobacco. She climbed in to retrieve it.

"Get outta here!" Homer sneered.

Angie mustered up her courage and said, "I want my blanket."

"I said, get outta here," Homer warned her.

"Give me my blanket," Angie set her jaw.

After Homer gave her a long deadly look, he finally said, "First Elmer, now you."

He relented and pulled the blanket out from under him and tossed it to her. "Now, go away."

She reached over and grabbed her blanket, retreating out the back of the wagon as quickly as she could.

"Why's he so mean?" Margaret asked Angie.

"Don't know," Angie shrugged her shoulders, "he just is."

"Maybe a girl broke his heart and he can't get over her." Margaret suggested.

Again Angie shrugged her shoulders.

"Where'd you get the blanket?" Margaret changed the subject, "Did your mother make it for you?"

"No," Angie shook her head, "I made it."

"You're telling me a fib," Margaret laughed, "I can tell."

Angie shot her a look and said, "I did too make it! My mother taught me how last winter. I was going to enter it in the Boone County Fair and win a blue ribbon but my family died and now I have to go to California, so I couldn't enter it. But I'm going to enter it in the fair in Sacramento and I'll win a blue ribbon, you'll see!"

The smile left Margaret's face and she was quiet. Finally she said, "I'm sorry, Angie. I didn't mean to make you mad. Your blanket is really pretty."

"Thank you," Angie quietly responded.

"Will you teach me how to make a blanket too?" Margaret asked.

Angie shook her head no.

After many minutes of silence, Margaret said, "Well, I guess I'm gonna go see what my mother's doing. She might need my help."

Angie nodded but still didn't say anything.

Margaret was sad as she walked back over to her camp, wondering what had happened.

That night, no one spoke. The Smith camp was quiet and everyone retired early.

Angie lay in bed and prayed, *God, I miss them so much it hurts, especially my momma. I need her really bad. Please send her back to me. Please send them all back to me. I hate it here without them. Why couldn't I have died too? Then I could be with them and we could all be happy.*

Tears began to stream down her face for the first time in a long time. She buried her head in her pillow and clung tight to her blanket. Soon she felt an unexplainable peace flow through her and her tears began to ease. The grace of sleep began to overtake her and she drifted off with images of her mother flowing through her dreams.

****

CHAPTER NINE

The River

When the word of Cholera spread throughout the camp, people began to panic. Two families had reported members being taken with the illness and fell toward the back of the train. The other travelers were clamoring for space between them and the sickness, fearing for their own families. Cholera was a death sentence for nine out of ten people who were stricken with it. Wagon Master Taylor had to ask the families with the disease to stay behind in order to keep the rest of the wagon train healthy. If able, they could travel a day's distance behind and those that survived the disease could travel with Wagon Master Billings' group when they caught up with them.

Before the wagon train had time to move on without them, one of the stricken travelers was already dead. The train moved on, side by side, in order to keep the dust from kicking up in each other's faces. The prairie was wide and sparse and provided plenty of room to spread out.

An evening meeting was called for all travelers. "We'll be crossing one more river," the wagon master informed the emigrants, "and this one's worse than the last one. The Green

River is the most difficult to cross and we'll be crossing by ferry again. We're heading up to the Names Hill Ford ferry and should be arriving in a couple days. Be prepared to wait in line again. Because of the difficulty of the crossing, I hear they've been charging $20.00 per wagon, for everybody, no exceptions."

"Ain't there anyplace else we can cross?" one man asked.

"You have your choice of going farther upstream to Red Buttes. It's a might dangerous. Lots of people have drowned there, but that's the only other place to cross," Bishop offered.

When Homer returned to the camp, he informed Elmer, "We're headin' for Red Buttes. We'll be leavin' the wagon train and takin' a faster route."

"Leavin' the wagon train?!" Elmer exclaimed, "Homer! What are ya thinkin'?"

"I'm thinkin' that we ain't gonna spend any more time waitin' on ferries," he answered his brother. "We's already wasted too much time as it is. We ain't stupid. Don't take much brains to follow a trail. We just keep headin' west and we'll be there in no time. Besides, the snows gonna fall any time up there in those mountains just ahead. Don't want to get caught in it. Wait a few more days and that just might be what we'll be facin'."

"I don't know, Homer," Elmer hesitated, "We may be jumpin' the gun here."

"Ain't doin' no such thing," Homer assured him, "you'll see. I'll be tellin' the wagon master our intensions in the mornin'."

"Well, alright," Elmer agreed. "Just long as we keep to the trail."

Elmer felt as though he had a pit in his stomach and knew in his heart this may be a bad decision, but he was tired of fighting with Homer. He was worn down and tired and felt he may have already pushed Homer too far.

The next morning, Homer promptly informed the wagon master of his decision.

"Suit yourself," Bishop Taylor said, "but I think you're making a big mistake."

"Ain't no mistake," Homer responded as he turned to leave. "Be in California long before you."

****

With Names Hill Ford within sight, the front of the wagon train began lining up at the edge of the river. As the Smith wagon continued past the wagons, Angie asked, "Where are we going?"

After Elmer explained to her Homer's plan, she protested, "Elmer, no!" and stopped in her tracks, "I want to stay with the wagon train! What about Margaret?!"

"Take a few minutes to say your goodbyes," Elmer instructed as he stopped the mules, "then we'll be on our way. Besides, ain't ya tired of the trip? We go it alone, we can be in Sacramento much sooner. You'll be sleepin' in a nice warm bed and I'll be on my way back to Gertie. Don't that sound good?"

Angie didn't answer. The idea was not setting well with her and she was having a hard time grasping what was actually happening.

"We ain't got time for this," Homer grumbled.

"It'll only take a few minutes," Elmer responded to his brother. He then turned to Angie and said, "Go on now, go say goodbye to your friend."

Angie ran and caught up with Margaret's wagon.

"I have to say goodbye," Angie told Margaret.

"Goodbye?" Margaret asked.

"We're leaving the wagon train and going to Sacramento on our own," Angie looked sullenly at the ground.

"But that's not safe!" Margaret argued.

Angie shrugged her shoulders and continued to look at the ground.

"You can come with us," Margaret offered, "I know it'll be alright with my parents."

"I wish I could," Angie said, "but I can't. I have to go with them." She looked over at Homer and Elmer waiting for her.

"But you're my best friend," Margaret's eyes started to fill with tears.

Angie smiled at the distraught girl in front of her. "It'll be alright. We'll see each other again in Sacramento. It can't be that big of a town. Just ask for the Bakers. Charity and Benjamin Baker. I'll be living with them."

Margaret nodded her head. "I will, I'll look for you as soon as we arrive."

The girls gave each other a hug and then Angie ran back to her wagon. As they continued away from the wagon train, Angie struggled with her emotions and tried not to look back at Margaret.

She could hear the wagon master calling a muster and she turned to see people gathering at the riverside. She felt panic run through her body as they walked farther and farther away, and looked at Elmer and Homer, hoping they would change their minds. But the realization slowly settled in that they would not be going back to the wagon train. Again, she felt her security being threatened. And again, the overwhelming feeling of loneliness consumed her.

"It'll be alright," Elmer assured her, noticing her dismay, "It'll be just fine."

****

The Rocky Mountains were looming large in front of them as they began seeing more and more trees and green grass.

"We should be comin' up on the crossing point soon, within the next couple hours the way I figure it," Homer told Elmer.

"You been thinkin' how we're gonna get across that river?" Elmer asked.

"Can't be that hard," Homer answered, "Others have crossed there lots of times."

"An' others have drowned there, lots of times," Elmer added, being careful not to let Angie hear his concern.

"You been mighty uppity lately," Homer glanced over at his brother, "You think you know more than me?"

"Sometimes, I think I do," Elmer responded.

"Don't challenge me, Elmer," Homer threatened, "I've a mind to put you in yer place as it is! I think after we get this girl delivered to her folk, you and me best go our separate ways. Don't want to come to blows with you, Elmer, but it seems to be headin' thataway."

"Seems to me that might be best too," Elmer agreed, "I'm gonna head back to Missouri, see if Gertie will marry me anyhow."

Homer shot Elmer a sharp glare and then said, "Sometimes, I think you were born with only half a brain, Elmer. No woman is worth marryin'."

"Well, that's where I differ from you," Elmer smiled to himself, "I think Gertie is, and I think she just might have me."

"She'll just leave ya, just like ma did," Homer told him.

"Yeah, well, don't forget, pa left too," Elmer added. "But Gertie's different. She didn't leave her man. He went and died on her. She's true blue. I just know she is!"

"Not worth the pain and sufferin'," Homer shook his head, "You'll regret it. Ya can't even trust family!"

The closer they neared the river, the colder the air became.

"After we cross the river, we'll head straight for Fort Hill, Idaho and then along the Humbolt River through Nevada and we'll be in California in a couple weeks. Sacramento about a week after that," Homer thought out loud.

"Three more weeks," Elmer said thoughtfully.

"Better than that if we can push the mules a little harder," Homer suggested, "Travel a few more hours a day."

Elmer nodded his head, "Should be able to do that."

"Are you really going to go back to Missouri?" Angie asked Elmer.

"Where'd you hear that?" Elmer asked her.

"I heard you talking to Homer," Angie answered, "You want to go back and marry Gertie."

"Well, ain't you got big ears," Elmer smiled. "Yep, I'm headin' back just as soon as we get our money from this here trip."

"If I don't like my aunt and uncle, can I come with you?" Angie asked.

"Come with me?" Elmer looked surprised, "Why on earth would ya want to do that?"

"I miss Elma and George," she answered, "I want to go back home."

"Sacramento's gonna be yer home," Elmer said gently.

"Please?" Angie begged, "Please promise me?"

"Well, we'll just have to see when we get there, won't we," he answered her, but not promising anything.

The rain began to come down, just a sprinkle but it was enough to dampen Homer's attitude.

"That's all we need," Homer fumed, "more mud."

"There's the river," Elmer said as they approached the Green River. It was overrun with water rushing over huge boulders, "This must be Red Butte. Where we gonna cross?"

"Seems like a good spot down there," Homer pointed a little farther upstream.

"The water seems a little high," Elmer said as he studied the river, "Moving awful fast."

"Aw, not that fast," Homer scowled at Elmer, "Come on, let's get this wagon across."

When they arrived at the spot that Homer had chosen, Elmer yelled over the sound of the rushing water, "Angie, get in the wagon! You'll be safer in there!"

She did as Elmer told her to, and Homer climbed onto the front of the wagon to drive it across. Elmer agreed to tread water and lead the mules by their bridles, just in case they spooked.

"If it gets too deep, just climb up on one of them mules," Homer instructed. Elmer nodded in agreement.

"Git up!" Homer yelled at the mules. They hesitated but Homer kept driving them forward with Elmer pulling on their bridles, "Come on ya stubborn beasts, move!"

The mules were strong and pulled away, put Homer and Elmer fought with them until they began to move out into the river. The deeper they went into the water, the more the mules began to become alarmed. The strength of the water pushed them off balance and the slippery rocks under their hooves only added to the turmoil. Elmer struggled to keep on his feet as he fought to keep the mules moving forward. Homer kept yelling at the mules and the wagon was rocking violently in the river. Angie began to get scared and soon became frozen with fear.

In the middle of the river, the mules lost their footing, reared up and began braying in panic. They pulled away from Elmer and thrashed through the water. Elmer yelled for help as he was washed downstream, with Homer losing grip of the reins.

Angie knew they were in trouble, and could hear the wood of the wagon cracking and breaking. The water under the wagon was beginning to shake the wagon violently and move it swiftly through the rapids. There was no more control and she felt helpless feeling the wagon hit the boulders along the river.

As the wagon began to break up, Angie called out, "God help me! Please help me!"

Her blanket was close by, so she grabbed it and pressed it close to her for comfort.

The next thing she knew, the wagon was tipping over and onto its side. She screamed as the water began rushing inside. The canopy tore from the ribs of the wagon and possessions began to pour into the river.

She felt the water trying to suck her out of the wagon. Noise from the wood breaking all around her was deafening along with the sound of rushing water. She was being tossed around forcibly as what was left of the wagon spun and twisted through the river. She fought to keep her head above water and held onto the side of the wagon with one hand and her blanket with the other. Through her screams she kept praying for help. Suddenly, the river began to ease, and then she realized that she was drifting, holding onto only a few boards, what was left of the back of the wagon. Then she felt herself stop, the wood caught between several boulders on the side of the river.

It took her a few minutes to catch her breath and to realize that she had reached the shore unscathed. She dragged her blanket, heavy with water, upon one of the boulders and then used all the strength she had left to pull herself out of the water and on top of another boulder.

She looked around her as she waited for her heart to stop pounding. All she could see was the wreckage from the wagon and most of their belongings washing away with the currents.

Where was Homer and Elmer? Where were the mules?

"There you are!" she heard from behind her.

It was Homer, walking down the bank toward her.

"Come on, help me collect these here boards," Homer ordered, "We need to make a raft."

"Why?" Angie questioned.

"Cause the mules are on the other side of the river, ya dumb girl, and we've gotta go get 'em," Homer answered, frustrated and drenching wet.

"Where's Elmer?" Angie asked.

"Last I seen him he was bein' washed down river."

"We need to find him!" Angie became alarmed.

"No sense in doin' that. He's long gone by now." Homer told her.

"But he may need our help!" Angie tried to reason with Homer.

"Don't be stupid, girl," Homer snarled, "If the rocks haven't killed him, the currents surely have!"

"Don't you care about Elmer?" Angie argued. "He's your brother!"

"Don't do no good to get emotional," Homer was getting even more agitated, "Can't bring him back. Come on now, help me get these boards."

Angie shook her head 'no' and refused to move.

"You stupid, stupid girl!" Homer was extremely irritated by now, "If I wasn't to get the other half of my money when I get you to California, I'd leave you here to die!"

"Go ahead!" Angie challenged him as she picked up her wet blanket and carefully made her way over the boulders and onto the shore.

"Just shut yer trap and help me," Homer ordered.

"Help yourself because I'm not going to help you!" Angie said as she found herself a place to sit down.

"Why, you little brat! You're tryin' my patience!" Homer was furious, "You need a good paddlin' and I'm just the one to give it to ya!"

"I'm not afraid of you," Angie set her jaw and looked stubbornly away from his stare.

Homer grunted, "You'll get yours later" and then angrily began dragging the boards he could reach out of the water.

After he had an ample collection of wooden planks, Homer began to look around for something to tie the boards together with.

Angie could see four of the mules farther on down the other side of the river grazing on fresh grass with the tongue of the wagon still attached to the back of them. Everything else had been washed down the river, including the fifth mule. She hoped that Elmer and the mule survived and that they found each other, and Elmer was riding to meet up with the wagon train.

Homer swore as his frustration grew trying to find vines or anything that would suffice as rope.

Suddenly, his face lit up as he spotted Angie's blanket.

"That'll do!" Homer said as he approached her and snatched up the blanket.

"What are you doing?" Angie feared as she grabbed for her blanket.

Homer took out his pocket knife and cut the end stitch and began to unravel the knots.

"Stop it! Don't do that! You're ruining my blanket!" Angie screamed as she tried to pull the blanket from his grasp.

Homer shoved Angie down onto the ground while retaining the blanket in his grasp. As he continued to unravel the blanket even more, he said, "Don't give me no more trouble, ya hear? We need this here yarn to tie up the raft. You can have it back when we reach the other side of the river."

"I hate you for what you're doing! That's all I have left of my family!" Angie yelled at him.

"Don't make no difference to me whether ya hate me or not," Homer responded. "What's gotta be done, has gotta be done."

Angie refused to help Homer bind the boards together with her yarn. She would only sit and glare at him. Her many months of working hard on her blanket, her blessings, all unraveled, all gone. She ached inside and wanted to cry but she was too angry to cry.

"Come on," Homer said when he launched the raft into the water, "Get on. The river's pretty peaceful here. We should have no trouble gettin' to the other side."

Angie got up and gathered up what yarn Homer had not used and then boarded the raft, sitting down on the front as Homer sat toward the back of the raft, using a fairly long plank to row with.

No words were exchanged as Homer steered the handmade raft to the other side, just down from where the mules were eating. One mule looked up at them with curiosity and then went back to eating.

"Come on, girl. Let's get them mules and find the trail. Maybe we can find the wagon train again. With no wagon to pull, we should be able to make good time and catch 'em," Homer said. "Got no food or water. We'll need the wagon train to help us now."

Angie knelt down to untie her yarn.

"Whatcha doin'?" Homer became irritated again.

"Getting my yarn," Angie answered as she began untying the string from the boards.

"We don't have time for that you stupid girl! We gotta unhitch these mules and catch that wagon train!" Homer said impatiently.

"Not without my yarn," Angie continued to untie each board. "You said I could get my yarn when we got to the other side."

Homer grabbed Angie by the arm and yanked her to her feet.

"Come on!" Homer began to drag her away from the raft.

But Angie began pulling away in the other direction trying to reach the raft, yelling at the top of her lungs, "No, let me go! You said I could have my yarn! Let go of me!"

The Blanket of Blessings 161

The ruckus caught the attention of two Shoshone braves who had been out hunting. The yells of the little girl sounded like cries for help and the Indian men rode their horses down the bank of the river until they came to the opening where they saw a white man pulling a little girl against her will. They assumed she was in trouble and approached Homer and Angie.

Homer was startled to see them and exclaimed, "Injuns!"

He pulled his knife out of his pocket and threw back his arm in an attempt to throw the knife at the two strangers, but one of the braves was able to toss his spear before Homer could release his knife. The spear hit Homer square in the chest, taking Homer down to the ground. As Homer fell, he lost his grip on Angie's arm and she ran immediately back to the raft and began untying her yarn from around the boards again.

One of the Indians dismounted his horse and checked Homer, only to find him dead, and then they both looked at Angie feverishly gathering her yarn. They looked at each other with surprise and were puzzled at the little girl's behavior. Was she crazy?

The brave who was still standing next to the dead white man went over to Angie, knelt down and began to help her untie and gather the yarn. He did not understand her fierce desire for this colored string, but he knew it was important to her and he would help her. She looked at him gratefully as she continued her work. The other brave covered Homer's body with branches, leaves and dirt.

As Angie stood up with her arms holding huge heaps of yarn, the Shoshone braves helped her gather the last of her yarn and walked her to their horses. Angie somehow knew she must go with them and never questioned the thought as survival was her only concern now. She rode behind one of the braves, the other brave leading the unhitched mules behind his horse.

As they rode along the river, Angie looked back at where she last saw Homer. She hadn't fully comprehended yet the fact that he was dead, and that Elmer was probably dead as well. She looked at her huge armload of wet yarn in front of her and the long black hair running down the back of the man in front of her. Again, that feeling of familiarity, combined with the feeling of unfamiliarity was overwhelming her.

She then became aware of the cold against her wet clothes, causing her to shiver. She wished her blanket was dry and whole again. She wanted to wrap it around her and feel its warmth one more time.

My blessings, she thought, *All my blessings are gone. I've got to put them back together again. I will, I promise you momma. I'll crochet the blanket back together and put all the blessings back into it. And it will keep me warm.*

****

CHAPTER TEN

The Village

As they rode through the trees of the forest, Angie's clothes began to dry, but her feet were still wet in her boots. The sun shone through the leaves and she heard birds singing, for the first time since she left Missouri, maybe because the rattle of wagon wheels and the activities around the campfires didn't drown them out anymore.

The two men talked in a strange language that confused her, but she didn't feel threatened, more interested than anything else. She saw two dead rabbits hanging across the back of one of the horses, and a small deer strapped across one of the mules. She supposed the rider she was with had been carrying the deer before they came across her. After many weeks of beans, hard tack and coffee, the fresh meat looked inviting to her. Over a spit, it would taste really good.

Approaching a clearing in the trees, a green plush valley appeared before them with a small river winding through the middle of it. A large number of teepees spotted one side of the river in among a large grove of trees. Some had campfires ablaze in front of their homes and the smoke billowed through the trees drifting into the air above. Horses grazed in the nearby pastures with dogs and laughing children running through fields of wildflowers and stalks of corn.

As the horses made their way down a small incline toward the river, the dogs began to bark uncontrollably, alerting the village of someone coming near. Angie was fascinated by what she saw; it was truly a whole new world to her. It seemed so peaceful and serene, and a feeling of awe came across her.

As they entered the village, activities began to cease as people turned to stare at her. She suddenly felt conspicuous and wanted to hide behind the man in front of her. They stopped at one teepee and both men climbed down from their horses, with her rider holding his hand up to let her know to stay where she was. Then, they disappeared inside the teepee. She looked all around her and noticed she had become the center of attention and she felt herself sink on top of the horse. Soon another man came out of the teepee with the other two, a much older man with silver streaks in his hair and hard features. He looked up at her, and the three continued their conversation. Angie wished she knew what they were saying. Finally, the tall man with the kind face climbed back on the horse in front of her. He took the lead of one of the mules they had brought back with them, turned and went over to a teepee close to the river where an old woman was sitting on the ground grinding corn.

The man jumped down and after a few minutes of exchanging words, the man began to walk away. He then tied the lead for the mule to a nearby tree and took Angie down from the horse. After a few words to her, he started to lead his horse away. Angie began to follow him but he turned and held up his hand, said a few more words and pointed to the old woman. Angie stayed where she was as she watched him walk away, blending into the village.

The old woman looked up at Angie holding her armload of colored string, and a frown came over her wrinkled face.

Angie was about to say something, when suddenly, the overwhelming odor of skunk penetrated the area as a boy, not much older than herself, came stomping into the village. He was obviously angry and his mixed breed dog trotted sheepishly beside him. As his eye caught sight of Angie, he stopped in his tracks and examined her from head to foot several times. The smell became more than Angie could bear and she stepped back and wrinkled her nose, infuriating the curious boy. He let out a grunt and glared at Angie as he continued to stomp past her. The villagers began to laugh and point at him, and Angie wished she could understand them.

Soon, a shriek could be heard from the other side of the village and Angie smiled as she saw the boy being escorted by his mother's grasp to the river and she shoved him in. Angie joined in the laughter when the dog went in the water behind him. The old woman looked disapprovingly at Angie, but she didn't utter a sound. The smile left Angie's face as the old woman pointed for her to sit down.

Angie obediently did so and the old woman grabbed the huge piles of yarn from Angie's arms and tossed them aside. She then picked up a rock called a corn pounder and began to show Angie how to grind corn on a large worn rock. She then handed the long rock to Angie and barked some orders to her. Angie didn't understand her, but she knew what the old woman wanted and began to grind the corn the best she could. The old woman became short of patience and shoved Angie's hands down with her withered old fingers, showing Angie the proper way to grind corn. The old woman voiced her instructions in unintelligible sounds to Angie.

I'm not going to cry, Angie vowed, *I'm strong like my daddy and I am not going to cry, not ever again!*

This had become Angie's official introduction to Halona, the old woman whom she would come to live with. Halona made Angie work hard every day and never broke a smile. She seemed angry inside and had a very short temper. Angie felt as though she was always in Halona's way and that Halona was irritated to have her living with her. No one came to visit with the old woman and she seemed to like it that way.

In the evenings, after dinner, Angie would sit around the campfire and roll her yarn into different colored balls. Halona just shook her head and thought the girl to be crazy. Angie spent any free time she had washing the yarn and hanging it to dry. The villagers were curious about her many "colors of string" but no one touched it, as it seemed strange to them. All except Kimana, a friendly girl of Angie's age. She loved to touch the yarn and helped Angie wash it clean. She was the first girl Angie had befriended in her new home.

Within the next several weeks, Angie came to recognize most of the children in the village and began to learn their names.

There was Chocheta, a happy girl who liked to talk a lot. Angie couldn't understand her of course, but Angie knew that Chocheta was very friendly and that she liked her. Chocheta was pretty with beautiful shiny hair that was carefully combed and arranged by her mother.

And there was Leotie, another girl around the same age as herself, who was very shy and would follow behind her friends everywhere they went. She was somewhat stout with pretty eyes and braided hair.

And of course there was Kimana and Angie liked her best. She was the oldest of four children, with a younger sister, a younger brother, and a baby brother who was just born to her parents. She was kind and gentle and very patient with Angie. She was taller than Angie, had long black eyelashes, golden brown eyes, and a smile that warmed her face. Kimana and Angie were very curious about each other and spent most of their free time together.

Angie often saw Enyeto, the 12-year-old boy who had made such a surprising and odious impression on her first day in the village. His embarrassing predicament made him resent Angie and he teased her and tried to embarrass her as often as he could. He was slender and his long hair blew freely in the wind.

He also had several friends he led around the village. Elsu seemed more mature for his age, with deep brown eyes and a quiet way about him, with a kind face. His thick hair hung in a braid down the middle of his back with a scalplock twisted on the top of his head, and an eagle feather stuck through it. Maybe his maturity came from being the Chief's son, and more was expected of him.

Siwili was Leotie's older brother. He was more immature and he liked to be the center of attention, without much thought to the consequences that were sure to follow. He had a roundish face and his hair was pulled back tightly against his neck, hanging back in one long tail.

Angie soon learned that her daily duties were to feed and care for the mule and some wild prairie chickens, wash clothes and cooking pots and utensils, and to help prepare food. But her favorite chore was to chase the crows from the maize fields. Together with Kimana, Chocheta, and Leotie, Angie would run and yell at the top of her lungs in and among the stalks of corn, waving their arms wildly, letting go of as much frustration and anger as she could.

"Go away!" she would yell, thinking all the time the black bird was Enyeto.

"Get out of here!" she screamed, this time she imagining it was Halona.

"Don't come back!" to her imaginary Pearl as she waved her fist at the soaring crows above her.

She would run and run and yell until she was exhausted. It felt so good to then rest in the green grass and feel almost peaceful. To stare up into the sunlit sky and watch the clouds drift slowly by. She'd dream about better days, days with her mother and father. Days when she would play games chasing Billy around the yard and hearing her mother's voice as she put blessings into the stitches of her blanket.

One morning, after their early meal, Angie had returned from the river to find Halona busily tearing down their teepee and packing it onto a drag sled, two long poles covered by animal hides. She motioned for Angie to pick up some things and bring them to her. Angie realized that everywhere she looked, the women of the village were doing the same as Halona.

There was a frigid cold in the air this morning and people were moving very quickly to accomplish their tasks. The poles with all their belongings were soon attached to the mule that had been given to Halona and it was not long when everyone was ready to leave the valley. Some families attached their drag sleds to their dogs that were eager to help with the move.

Halona knelt down and pulled out an animal hide and wrapped it around herself to keep warm during their journey. She glanced up at Angie and then turned to pull out a smaller hide and handed it to Angie reluctantly. Angie smiled at Halona and wrapped it around her, but the old woman just stood up, and walked to the front of the mule, pulling it along with a rope behind her. Angie had the strange feeling of being back with the wagon train, only this time, there was no wagon for comfort.

The men had joined and several hundred Shoshone began the trek to the Plains for the winter. Angie didn't understand where they were heading, only that they were taking her with them. Halona didn't seem to mind if Angie was out of sight, so Angie spent most of her time walking with Kimana, who was trying to explain to Angie why they were moving. With the language barrier, the girls were both frustrated, but attempted to communicate anyway. Angie learned a few words along the way, but most of the time was not interested in exerting herself to learn the new language. She was more insistent on trying to teach Kimana the English language, which Kimana struggled with as well.

In the evenings, the natives would sit around campfires to warm themselves, and sleep out in the open, wrapped up in hides and blankets. During the day, they would move on steadily south. Angie was impressed how quickly everyone moved, the people, the horses, mules, and dogs, taking everything they owned with them.

Soon the air felt warmer and the ground became dryer, with fewer and fewer trees. Wide open fields lay before them and the sun started to beat down on them relentlessly. The blankets and hides were tied to their poles and drug along behind them, leaving long ruts through the dirt.

Late one afternoon, Angie could see off in the distance the smoke of many campfires. Another large village of Shoshone people lived along another stretch of river out on the plains with no protection from trees. Just scrub brush and sagebrush lay all around. The last of a corn harvest was being gathered for the winter.

As the front of the line started to enter the village, people all gathered around to welcome the new arrivals. There was much laughter and happiness as all began talking and sharing news. Angie supposed they must be relatives and it felt like Christmas had come, a time for celebration and merriment. She was anxious to finish her journey and ran up to walk along Halona into the village. Then, that same uncomfortable feeling began to overwhelm her again as the people from the new village stopped talking and began to stare at her. Her blonde hair and blue eyes stood out among the people wherever she was. She ignored them and walked alongside the old woman until Halona found a place she was satisfied with, to set up her teepee. Angie tried to help Halona, but felt she was more of a hindrance than a help. Halona kept pushing her aside and went about setting up her teepee all on her own. Angie was amazed at how efficient Halona was at her task. Angie could see that Halona had done this chore many times before and she knew it was best to just stay out of her way.

She sat on the ground and petted a stray dog that had come to her for some attention. After the dog went on his way, Angie picked herself up and went to find Kimana. She found Chocheta's family first, already set up and preparing a campfire. When Chocheta's mother saw her, she motioned for Angie to come over to their teepee. Chocheta's mother, Amitola, was very vain, and very beautiful. She smiled at Angie, and had her sit down.

She pulled out a comb, and sat down behind Angie, and gently began to comb Angie's tangled hair. Amitola knew that Halona was not interested in helping Angie with her grooming, and that Angie was left on her own to take care of herself. She decided that she would help in that regard and took great pride in fixing Angie's hair into a beautiful long braid down the middle of her back.

Chocheta sat beside Angie and showed her the dolls her mother had made her when she was a little girl. Angie held one and was amazed at how intricate the beadwork was on the dolls dress. She tried to tell Chocheta how beautiful the dress was, but became frustrated when her words were not understood. Finally, Angie smiled, nodded at Amitola, and then left to find Kimana.

By late afternoon, Angie found each of her friends' campsites and wandered back to her teepee to help prepare their evening meal.

"See my hair," Angie said to Halona, stroking her braid.

Halona looked at her, shook her head, and went back to grinding corn. Then she handed the corn pounder to Angie and went into the teepee, leaving Angie to sit alone, wondering why Halona was so mean. Why couldn't she be like Amitola? She was nice and seemed to care about her. Why were there so many mean people in the world? Pearl, Homer, and now Halona. But there were good people in the world too, and she would try her best to be like them and to be kind to others, the way her mother tried to teach her to be.

How she missed her mother. She wished it had been her mother combing her hair today instead of Amitola. Speaking kind words of encouragement and kissing her on the top of her head. Would she ever stop missing her mother? She guessed not.

I'll never stop missing my mother; she thought to herself, *I will always need my mother.*

****

CHAPTER ELEVEN

The Name

That night, when Angie retired for bed, she looked for her yarn to hold it to her as she usually did, but couldn't find it. She looked all through the teepee for it but to no avail. Angie became frantic and began to tear her bedding apart. Halona stopped her and began rambling off in the Shoshone language that Angie had been ignoring for over a month, except for learning a few words from Kimana. Realizing that Halona had done something with her yarn, Angie knew that the only way to find out what happened to it was to learn to speak Shoshone, and that is exactly what Angie set in her mind to do.

Angie had a fitful night and couldn't sleep, worrying that Halona may have thrown away her yarn or left it behind in the mountains. The next morning she searched all around their campsite, inside the teepee and outside, but still no sight of her yarn. She had to find her yarn, and she set her jaw just as she saw her father do so many times before.

I won't give up, she told herself. *It has to be here somewhere!*

Angie listened to every word that was spoken in the village, and with Kimana and Chocheta's help, she began to catch on to the language at a feverish pace. Every day and night she thought about her yarn, almost obsessively and it drove her to the point of practicing her new language exclusively, letting her English fade with the days, weeks and months.

Halona was amused at Angie's grasp of her native tongue, but only called her a "silly girl" and criticized her pronunciation of the language.

Angie soon became fluent in the Shoshone language. Every day Angie would ask Halona for her yarn, but the old woman would say, "Cannot understand you."

One day Angie told her in her best Shoshone wording, "You can understand me. You are choosing to ignore me, I will keep asking every day until you tell me where it is. I will not stop asking, ever!"

After a long silence, Halona relented and said, "The colored string is mine. Everything in teepee is mine. It is put away. If you want it, you must earn it. Then I will give it to you."

"What do I need to do to earn it?" Angie asked.

"I will know, and you will know," she answered. Halona refused to discuss it any further.

Angie was frustrated, but at least she had the hope of getting her yarn back.

****

As Angie turned 12 years old, at least she was fairly certain that the month of February had come and gone, she had become fairly sufficient at learning the Shoshone language. She also realized that Halona had given her an Indian name. Sometimes Halona would call her Tsomah Sadzi, but most of the time, she would just call her Tsomah. Angie asked Halona what the name "Tsomah" meant, as she knew by now that all Shoshone names have a meaning to them. Halona just said, "It is your name, do not bother me with nonsense."

The next day when Angie went to the river, she saw her friend Kimana playing with her baby brother. She asked Kimana what the name Tsomah Sadzi meant. Kimana laughed a little and then asked, "Where did you hear this name?"

"Halona calls me that name," Angie answered.

"Tsomah means 'yellow hair' and Sadzi means 'with disposition'.

"I do not like it," Angie frowned, "I don't like it at all. She should call me by my real name...Angie Owens."

Enyeto was nearby fishing and overheard them. "I like your Shoshone name," he smiled, "She has given you a good name. From now on I will call you Tsomah."

"My hair is not yellow, it is blonde. And my name is Angie!" she insisted, "Angie Owens! I will not answer to any other name!"

"Tsomah! Tsomah! Tsomah!" Enyeto taunted Angie.

"Come," Kimana picked up her brother and took Angie's arm leading her away from the river, "Walks as a Bear does not know his place."

"Walks as a Bear?" Angie asked, confused, as the girls walked beside the water.

"That is his name. Enyeto means 'Walks as a Bear'."

"What does your name mean?" Angie asked Kimana.

"Butterfly," Kimana answered.

"Just Butterfly?" Angie questioned.

"Yes," Kimana smiled.

"What does Leotie mean?" Angie's curiosity grew.

"Flower of the Prairie," Kimana answered.

"And Chocheta?" Angie continued.

"Welcome Stranger," Kimana replied.

Angie thought for a moment and said, "And Halona…what does Halona mean?"

"Of Happy Fortune," Kimana said quietly.

"Of Happy Fortune?!" Angie was surprised, "she does not seem happy to me."

"Once she was happy," Kimana explained, "I have been told that when she was young, she was very pretty and she married one of the handsomest braves in our village. His name was Motega, which means 'New Arrow'. They were not given children, but she was still happy as they were very much in love. Her husband became an elder in the village and was a very important man. His position made her proud and she found her worth in this man and for many years she felt important among our people. About two years ago, a wagon train came through our land. Motega went with many other braves to trade goods with the wagon train. After they returned, some men became very ill. Motega was one of them and died two days later. Halona lost everything, her husband, her standing in the village, and her joy. She blames the white man for her husband's death, for bringing their illness to our people."

"That is why she does not like me," Angie realized, "I can understand her coldness now."

"The elders decided to give you to her to replace her husband," Kimana went on to explain, "to ease her loneliness."

"I can not replace her husband," Angie remarked, "I could never mean to her what her husband was to her."

"You will ease her pain, you will see. The elders know what is best."

"God knows what is best," Angie said staring out at the river, "My mother used to say that. God will turn all bad things into something good if we trust Him."

Kimana looked curiously at Angie, and then asked, "What does Angie Owens mean?"

"Mean?" Angie looked surprised, "That is just my name."

"My name is Kimana, and it means 'Butterfly'," Kimana insisted, "What does your name mean?"

Angie thought for a moment and then blurted out, "It means Princess of Columbia."

"What does the word 'Princess' mean?" Kimana asked her.

"Chieftain's daughter," Angie was pleased with her interpretation.

"Are you really a Chieftain's daughter?" Kimana's eyes grew large.

"Yes, from the Island of Columbia," Angie's bragging became exaggerated, "My father was the most important man in our town."

Soon the news spread throughout the camp that Angie was a chieftain's daughter from a white man's village a long distance away and Angie was not brave enough to correct them. The lie seemed to give her some respect, even though it didn't seem to faze Halona.

Several days later, Kimana and Leotie had joined Angie at the riverside to do their daily washing. They were laughing and telling secrets as all girls do.

Suddenly, Enyeto and Siwili ran toward them, smearing mud in Angie's face and hair, and then ran off laughing to each other.

As the girls helped Angie wash her hair and face, Angie asked them, "Why do they hate me so much? I have done nothing mean to them."

"I think they are afraid," Kimana answered.

"Afraid of what?" Angie responded surprised.

"Of different people. Of the changes coming to our land," Kimana explained, "Every Shoshone talks about it in the secret of their camps."

"But we do not want to hurt anyone," Angie objected.

"Fear always causes men to hurt each other," Kimana responded.

Angie's old rebellious nature was beginning to get the best of her. She turned to Kimana and Leotie and said, "I need your help."

"What are you going to do?" Leotie asked her, seeing that Angie's was cooking up some scheme in her mind.

"Enyeto and Siwili need to stop being mean to me," Angie told them, "I will show them what it feels like to be treated badly."

"I do not think that is wise," Kimana told her.

"Will you help me?" Angie asked Kimana.

Kimana hesitated a few moments, and then nodded her head.

The girls then spent the next hour planning out the details of Angie's revenge.

****

That night, the village was busy with their meals and entertaining friends and family from other tribes. Storytelling was rampant around the campfires and no one noticed Angie, Kimana and Leotie as they slipped away to meet by the river. Kimana's father was a craftsman and enjoyed creating and painting all kinds of artwork. From his supplies, Kimana was able to get several handfuls of porcupine quills that her father used in his crafts. Angie took a handful and then they quietly worked their way through the back of the village until they came to the back of Enyeto's family teepee.

Looking around and seeing no one, Angie carefully pulled up the hide of the teepee and slipped inside. Finding a nearby bed that she was sure belonged to Enyeto, she dumped the handful of quills into his bedding and then quickly made her departure before being spotted.

Siwili's family teepee was next to Enyeto's teepee, and after Kimana handed her the rest of the quills, Angie poured the remaining pointed needles in Siwili's bedding. The girls then quietly made their way back to the river. Once reaching the water, they could hold their giggling no longer and held their hands over their mouths as their laughter became out of control. They danced around, celebrating their success.

As the village was beginning to retire for the night, the three girls quietly made their way back to the scene of Angie's revenge.

"I will be in much trouble if my father knows I am here," Leotie told the girls.

"Halona will have my hide as well," Angie agreed. "We will hurry and be in bed before they find us gone."

The minutes seemed like hours as they waited for Enyeto and Siwili to enter their teepees. The boys continued talking outside their tents until finally Siwili's mother called him inside.

The girls held their breaths as they waited for the inevitable. It was only but a moment or two longer when they heard screams from inside both tents. The first to emerge was Siwili, holding his backside and yowling like an old dog. The next was not Enyeto, but his father, holding his posterior as well. Both were dancing around in front of their teepees while the mothers were trying to help them.

Their eyes were wide in shock when they saw Enyeto's father emerge from the tent. All three girls scurried back through the village, running for their own teepees.

"Oh no," Angie said as they ran, "Oh no!"

"We are in so much trouble!" Kimana agreed.

Angie stopped the girls. "It is our secret! No one say anything unless we are asked. Pray we will not be!"

The girls nodded and then nonchalantly walked back to their homes.

In bed that night, Angie prayed to God asking Him to forgive her and afraid of the possible repercussions.

The next day, the word in the village was that there must have been a stray porcupine or two, wandering through the teepees looking for food. The girls sighed with relief and were grateful not to have been caught.

When the newness of the incident had worn away, Angie forgot all about her prayer to God and her anger toward Enyeto returned. His continual taunting and snide remarks brought Angie's young foolishness to the surface again.

She saw her opportunity when she found Enyeto bathing with four other boys in the river.

"We cannot go over there!" Kimana told her. "We are not allowed to go near while they are bathing."

Angie marched right up to the edge of the river, much to the horror of the boys.

"Tsomah!" Enyeto yelled, "Go away!" The other boys also yelled for her to go.

Angie looked down on the shore and spotted the boy's clothes. Not knowing which were Enyeto's clothes, she gathered them all in her arms and turned to leave.

"No! No!" the boys screamed. "Bring them back!"

"You can blame Enyeto for this!" Angie called back to them as she ran from the river and out to the fields. Kimana was on her heals and telling her to take the clothes back, but she was determined to continue with her plan. She knew of a wasp's ground nest and threw the clothes on top of it.

"What have you done?" Kimana said in horror, "they will be so angry!"

"I am not afraid," Angie told her.

Kimana shook her head in disbelief, "I am your friend. I do not want to see you in trouble."

Angie started to think about what she had done. Again!

"What have I done, Kimana?" she asked her friend. "Why do I always get myself in trouble?"

"You think with your heart, not with your head," Kimana responded, "and your heart misled you."

They walked back to the village waiting for the results of Angie's actions. Again Angie was asking God for help. She knew that once Halona heard of what she had done, she would be in a lot of trouble.

Soon Chocheta ran to find Angie. She found her sitting with Kimana at Kimana's family teepee.

"Angie!" Chocheta said, out of breath. "The elders know what you did. They are discussing your punishment. Where are the clothes? The boys had to cover themselves with leafs to leave the river."

Kimana looked at Angie, and Angie looked at the ground. Remorsefully, she answered, "I threw them on the wasp's nest out in the field."

Chocheta looked horrified. "Maybe if you bring them back you won't be punished."

"I cannot," Angie said. "The wasps were swarming all over them."

"Maybe we should try," Kimana suggested.

Angie nodded her head and the girls walked back out to the field, with Chocheta joining them.

When they got to the pile of clothes, the wasps were still crawling on top of them, but not as many as before.

"What are we going to do?" Kimana asked.

"I'll get them," Angie told her, "I threw them there. I need to get the clothes back. Stay here. I don't want you to get stung."

Angie slowly and carefully approached the nest. Her heart beat so fast she thought she wouldn't be able to control it. The closer she got to the nest, the more her knees weakened and the more she shook. Before she could change her mind, she lunged for the clothes, grabbed them and began to run, with her friends running ahead of her. They were all screaming as the wasps began to swarm into a frenzy. Angie felt one sting after another as the girls ran down to the river. Angie threw the clothes down on the ground and the girls jumped into the water to avoid being stung any further.

"I'm so sorry," Angie told her friends, "I didn't want you to get hurt." The girls were frantically swatting the wasps away and still screaming.

It was but a few moments later when the elders and Chief Nahele came walking down to the shoreline, along with many of the villagers who wanted to see what the ruckus was all about.

The girls looked pathetic, but Angie got the worst of it, having many stings to show for it.

The chief smiled and turned to the elders. "She has been punished." They then turned and walked back to the village.

The boys were also among the crowd, laughing at Angie's predicament. Angie glared at Enyeto and her anger began to grow again.

Help me God! She seethed between her teeth, *Help me control my anger.*

****

It was only a few days later when Enyeto approached Angie while she was walking with her friends, their wasp stings still evident.

"Tsomah!" Enyeto chided her, "Tsomah!"

Angie clenched her jaw and responded, "My name is Angie Owens, not Tsomah!"

Enyeto was quiet for a moment as he followed behind them.

"Stop!" Enyeto demanded, "I want a white man's name. Give me a white man's name."

"No," Angie responded stubbornly.

"Give me a white man's name!" Enyeto continued, "You have a Shoshone name, I want a white man name, one that all white men will know me by!"

Angie stopped walking and faced Enyeto and stubbornly responded, "I said no!"

"I am boy, you are girl," Enyeto was just as stubborn. "You must do as I say!"

"Alright," she said, "let me think of a name."

Enyeto anxiously watched her face.

"Your new white man name will be…Pearl," she decided, "Pearl Stinkbody."

"Is that a good white man name?" Enyeto asked with excitement in his voice.

"The best name ever," she smiled, feeling as though she'd finally gotten her revenge.

Enyeto repeated his new name with much delight and was excited to tell the other boys in the village. He ran toward the village yelling behind him, "See, I told you, you are not very smart. I made you give me a white man's name!" And he began to laugh triumphantly to himself.

"I would also like a white name," Kimana turned to Angie with pleading eyes.

"Me also," Leotie begged.

Angie named Kimana 'Honey Bee' And Leotie 'Snuggle Bug'. Soon, other children from the village came to Angie asking for white names and she desperately searched her thoughts to come up with names from her past.

When word of the new names reached Chief Nahele's ears, he became unsettled at the thought and it was decided among the elders to put a stop to it. He called Halona to his tent and informed her that no Shoshone shall be known by a white man's name. She obediently returned to her teepee, sought out Angie who was in her underclothes, washing her worn pioneer dress in the river and slapped her across the face, saying, "Silly girl, you get me in trouble with Chief Nahele. You are bad girl. Can do nothing right." She grabbed the wet garment out of Angie's hands and tossed it aside. "No more white man names, no more white man clothes! You live with Shoshone! You be Shoshone now!"

Halona then turned and walked back to her camp. Angie sat stunned, not knowing whether or not she should pick up her dress lying in the dirt. She touched the side of her face that still stung from the slap and fought back tears. Clad only in her pioneer underclothes, she left her dress where it was and got to her feet.

Chocheta saw what had happened. As she walked up to Angie, she smiled and took Angie by the hand, leading her back to camp. There, Chocheta's mother went inside their teepee and came out with a Shoshone dress, a little worn, but soft and homemade.

Chocheta's older sister, Sisika, was anxious for Angie to try it on. It had been hers and she had outgrown it, hoping to give it to Chocheta soon. Now it was more important to give it to Angie. Sisika helped Angie to change clothes and everyone seemed to approve.

Angie and Chocheta ran to show Halona, but all the old woman did was grunt and turn back to her basket weaving.

Angie smiled at Chocheta and hugged her and the girls ran to the river to show Kimana and Leotie.

"You are Shoshone now," Kimana smiled.

Those words bothered Angie.

I don't feel like a Shoshone girl, she thought, *I still feel like a white girl named Angie Owens from Columbia, Missouri. Most of the people here are nice to me, but I don't really belong here. I belong where my family is, my real family. I need to get to California, to my aunt and uncle.*

Her dress was different on the outside, but she was still the same on the inside. The more she thought about Kimana's words, the more she struggled with her heritage, beginning to cling to it more than ever before.

****

CHAPTER TWELVE

The Celebration

It seemed like a long winter to Angie, but spring was here and the leaves had returned to the trees. Kimana told Angie that they would soon be returning to the mountains, but before they went, the Sun Dance celebration would be held.

The village swelled to several thousand as Shoshone tribes from different parts of Idaho, Oregon, Nevada and Utah made the journey to join in the celebration. The excitement and gathering reminded Angie of the county fairs in Columbia and she felt swept up in the festivities.

The men gathered around huge campfires, waiting for word of the coming of the bison. Buffalo was the mainstay for the plains people, and hunting arrived once in the spring and once in the fall, depending on the migration of the huge animals. The bison meat was the centerpiece of the celebration and the hunt had to be accomplished before the Sun Dance could begin.

Sometimes weeks would go by before the buffalo would make their appearance. During that time, the Shoshone began to collect poles for the dance hall. Branches from the trees would be used for the walls and roof, and the longest poles were selected to be placed in the center of a cleared space. Three black rings were painted near the top of the poles before placing them. These rings were called "wish rings" where the warriors could ask for special gifts from the Sun god, such as wealth, strength, many wives, or success in battle.

Once the dance hall was completed, the people would also take advantage of the gathering of tribes to arrange and perform marriages, show off new babies, and make individual decisions on whether to return to their home or move on to other lands.

It was not long before two mounted hunters rode into the village and declared that buffalo had been spotted across the plains. Men gathered their spears and mounted their horses. Women and children prepared the drag sleds and followed on foot, all except the very young and the very old. They stayed behind to keep the fires burning and help prepare for the bounty.

Each hunter would stay by his kill until his family arrived to cut up the meat. The women were very adept at removing the hide and meat, first from one side, and then the horsemen would turn the bison over with ropes and the women did the same on the other side.

Angie was invited to go with Kimana's family as Halona stayed behind. Angie was curious about the great hunt and was anxious to do something she hadn't experienced before. Onawa, Kimana's father, sat on his horse beside the fallen animal, proudly waiting for his family to come with the drag sled. Waneta, her mother began the process of removing the hide and was very adept at the job. Angie was amazed to see Kimana almost as capable as her mother. Other women from Kimana's family, her aunts and a cousin also helped in removing the hide and meat as they would also share the meat for their families. Angie was revolted by the process. The blood was making her sick, but she continued to watch. She wasn't quite sure why, she just couldn't take her eyes away from the operation. Kimana asked her if she wanted to help. At first, Angie shook her head 'no', but then moved in closer and asked Kimana what she should do. After Waneta cut the slabs of meat, she helped Kimana load them onto the sled. Once all the meat was loaded, the hide was thrown on top to protect it from insects, and then the women followed the husband back to the village.

Angie looked behind her at the women who were still waiting for their husbands to make their kill, and was glad that Onawa was a good hunter.

Kimana's family was one of the first to return with their meat, but soon, other families began to return with their bison as well. Angie stayed with Kimana's family and helped them hang the meat to dry. After a few hours, they took the slabs of meat down and put them between two stones and pounded them until they were tender, and then hung them up again. Angie worked all afternoon with them, and tried her best to pound and hang the meat. Waneta smiled at Angie and nodded her head, assuring her that she was doing a good job.

By the time for the evening meal, Waneta handed Angie a slab of meat to take to Halona for the celebration. Angie was excited to show Halona her donation to the festival for them, and ran all the way. Proudly, she held out her arms showing Halona the large slab of meat.

"Look, Halona," Angie smiled. "I have brought us meat for the celebration!"

Halona was sitting outside her teepee preparing food for their meal. "Hang it up," Halona said, no expression on her face, and pointed over to a nearby pole.

"I worked hard today," Angie told her as she tried to tie it to the poles the best she could, "I helped gather the meat and we hung it to dry and then we pounded it and hung it again."

"I have done it many times," was all Halona said.

Even if Halona wasn't impressed, Angie felt good about her accomplishments.

Within the next several days, the hunting was over and the celebration began. Only the men called upon the wish rings to bestow them their favors from the Sun god. They painted their bodies white and then marched twice in opposite directions around the inside of the dance hall. They were preceded by a holy man carrying a buffalo skull, representing the buffalo spirit and giving thanks to the Great Spirit. Once all the men had marched through the hall and cast their wishes upon the wish rings, they rested for the night.

The next morning, at sunrise, each man painted his body in bright colors, donned aprons of beaded designs, bracelets of porcupine quills around their wrists, and a cluster of bells around their ankles. The musicians started to play, both men and women began to sing a monotonous chant, and the dancing began. For three days and nights, the dancers ate no food or drank liquid, only resting for short periods, swaying back and forth to the music.

Every morning, the medicine men from each village would give prayers and rub rabbit feet on the pole, reaching up toward the wishing rings, and the music and dancing would continue.

Angie didn't understand the spiritual aspects of the ceremony. The people asking for annual blessings and their relationship with the buffalo spirit didn't make sense to her. She didn't understand the Indian people's worship of the Great Spirit or the Mother Earth, or any of their other gods. Her tender age kept her distracted with children's games and a young girl's dreams.

On the fourth morning, the women began to roast the bison meat on the spits they'd built, gathered roots and berries, and brought other foods that had been collected, and started preparing for the great feast. Angie stayed with Halona all morning, helping to prepare for the celebration. She worked hard and wished Halona would appreciate any thing she did, but not a word of gratitude came from Halona's mouth.

At noon on that fourth day, the tom toms ceased playing, people stopped chanting, and there was only silence in the village. Those men who had not already been overcome with exhaustion, staggered around and fell to the ground, to rest for the coming evening celebration.

At sunset came the feast, and the village began to rejoice. Gifts, including horses and wives, were exchanged. Angie felt this tradition was very repulsive. She could understand giving away horses, but not wives. Some of the men had many wives, especially the chiefs. This was new to her and hard to comprehend.

More marriages were performed, and more engagements were agreed upon between the men. The women had very little to say about the arrangements, and some marriages were settled upon at the birth of the girl child. Angie felt very disturbed for her friends. Kimana had shared with her that she had already been promised in marriage to a man named Dyami. He was ten years older than she was, and they would marry when she reached the age of 15 at the Sun Dance celebration.

"Do you love him?" Angie asked her.

Kimana laughed and said, "No, he is an old man."

"He is not old, just older than us," Angie reasoned.

"He looks old to me," Kimana confided.

"Why are you going to marry him if you do not love him?" Angie asked her.

"To have a man is a great source of pride," Kimana answered. "He will provide for me and our children, and I will paint pictures on our teepee of his great accomplishments."

Kimana seemed satisfied with her future, but Angie just shook her head.

"I will not marry," Angie said, "unless I love him. He must be just like my father, and be very handsome."

"Very few women can decide such things," Kimana told her. "Only the men know what is best."

"That is silly!" Angie argued. "Do you think Enyeto knows what is best? Or Siwili? Or even Elsu?

"They are young," Kimana told her, "they will learn. Wisdom comes with age."

"Wisdom comes to us all," Angie insisted, "man or woman. I will listen to my heart and I will listen to my God. He will tell me what man I will marry or not marry."

"Will you ask the Sun god for this favor?" Kimana asked her.

"No, I do not pray to the Sun god," Angie responded, "I pray to the only God, the God of Heaven. The God of the Bible."

"The white man's god?" Kimana asked her.

"Yes, the white man's god," Angie confirmed, "He cares for me and has kept me safe and will someday return me to my people."

"You cannot leave us, Angie Owens," Kimana protested. "Your god has brought you to us and you are Shoshone now. You belong here."

"No," Angie said gently. "My God will take me to California one day. I know it in my heart."

"Then I will pray to him that he will change his mind," Kimana resolved.

Angie didn't say anything further, but knew her mind and her heart were set. Even with all the festivities, this celebration did not bring her closer to the Shoshone people. If anything, it made her feel even more different than before. She longed to be in a church again, with a Bible in her hand. She longed to celebrate Christmas and Easter and even May Day around the May Pole. She longed to be sitting inside a warm farmhouse with a simple Thanksgiving dinner set on the table, her family and friends enjoying stories around the fireplace. These people weren't that much different than her own, with their celebrations and stories and love of family. But it wasn't the same, and she longed for similarity again.

Tomorrow they would pack up and head back for the mountains. The snow should be gone now and their summer home was waiting for them.

I will stay with these people, Angie said to God in her prayers that night. *I will make them my people for as long as you wish me to live with them. But I pray to go home, God. I pray to go home to my own people. Please hear my prayer, O God, please send me home.*

****

CHAPTER THIRTEEN

The Fishing Lesson

The trail was wet on the way back to the mountains. The spring rain refreshed the air and helped to bring color back to the hills.

Enyeto and Siwili enjoyed running behind the girls and pulling their hair or running ahead and jumping out behind trees as the girls passed by to startle them. Elsu was quickly growing tired of their antics and told them so.

"You act like little children," he scolded them.

"And you act like an old man," Enyeto laughed at Elsu.

The girls appreciated Elsu defending them and started walking with him the rest of the journey, hoping that Enyeto and Siwili would get discouraged if Elsu was with them. He talked about things that were way beyond his years and thoroughly bored Angie. Kimana, Chocheta and Leotie seemed to hang on his every word, which irritated Angie. She rolled her eyes and daydreamed about reaching their summer home, which succeeded in blocking out his voice.

The more Angie ignored him, the more Elsu tried to get her attention. Being only 12 years old, boys were more of a bother than anything else as far as Angie was concerned, and she couldn't imagine them ever being anything more.

The villagers were happy to see their homeland again. The river had changed course a little with the winter runoff, and left less ground to set up their teepees, but the area was still ample for the tribe. Halona found a spot not too far from her old location and set up camp. No one seemed to be possessive of one spot or another. The ground offered many favorable areas and before evening, campfires were lit, teepees set in place, and meals were being prepared. The new harvest needed to be planted within the next few days before the ground became too hard. An early night of rest was required in order to accomplish the task ahead of them.

Angie found that being back at the old camp, old feelings came with it. She remembered the last time she slept here, her yarn was next to her. The memories of the colored string came flooding back and her heart began to yearn for her blanket again. How long must she wait, what must she do? She had no idea. She grabbed a nearby fur and wrapped her arm around it, pretending it was her crocheted blanket. That old feeling of comfort returned to her.

Someday, it will be the real thing, she told herself. *Someday it will be my blanket, all crocheted and whole again, filled with blessings and keeping me warm.*

****

Working out in the maize field was back breaking, but none of the women complained. The daughters worked alongside their mothers, as they had done for years. The littlest girls spent time learning how to perform their future chores and were then allowed to run off and play with the old women.

The men had gone hunting to bring fresh food back to the village. Plenty of dried bison meat was brought back from the celebration, but would be a staple if no other food was found that day. The young men were sitting next to the river hoping to catch fresh trout for the spits over the fires.

Angie's hands were beginning to blister, but she refused to say anything. At the end of the day, Angie walked down to the river and let the cold water wash away the dirt and blood from her blisters. Her friends were alongside her and talking about the new puppies that were just born the night before, wondering how the mother dog was able to walk so far being heavy laden with her unborn pups.

"I wish I could have a dog," Angie said to no one in particular, "but Halona will not let me. She does not like dogs."

"A dog would be good for her," Kimana said, "She needs something to love."

Suddenly, Kimana realized how the words must have hurt Angie. She quickly added, "I did not mean that she does not have you. She has you to love."

"She does not love me," Angie said sadly, "and I am afraid she never will."

"It is good that we love you," Chocheta said and the girls hugged each other in one large embrace.

These girls had become Angie's family and she thanked God for them.

****

The summer days were long, the air was hot, and the women worked hard encouraging the ground to give life to their seeds. Angie would watch the boys fishing upstream while she was doing the washing downstream. She yearned to be fishing with them. It intrigued her to watch the fish fight while being drawn through the water. The fight for life and death, and the need to bring food home for the families. She wanted to be part of that contribution to the village. She knew that working with the crops was important. She knew she was helping to feed the village. But she wanted to experience the thrill of the struggle, between her and the fish. Could she bring in a trout, a large trout, and would Halona finally be proud of her?

She left her washing and walked up the shoreline to where the boys were. They looked up at her with inquisitive eyes.

"I would like to learn to fish," she bravely said to no one in particular, but all of them in general. "Will you teach me?"

The boys began to laugh among themselves.

"Stupid girl," Enyeto said. "Girls do not hunt, girls do not fish."

Angie wanted to push him in the river, but she restrained herself and challenged him, "Are you afraid that I will catch a bigger fish than you?"

Enyeto laughed again, "No one can catch fish as large as I can."

Elsu looked at Enyeto and said, "I will teach her."

Enyeto shot him a surprised look and his mouth fell open, struggling for the right words to say.

"Come tomorrow morning," Elsu said to Angie, "and I will teach you to fish."

"Thank you!" Angie smiled, "I will be here!"

She clasped her hands and ran back down to her washing, excited to learn the art of fishing.

Early the next morning, Angie ran down to the river, but Elsu was nowhere to be found. She looked up and down the shore and back up to the village, but no sign of Elsu. She sat down on the shore and pulled her knees up to her chest, laying her head down, despondent. Her disappointment began to overwhelm her and anger began to grow inside of her.

"Stupid boys," she muttered. "You cannot trust them. They tell you one thing and then they do just the opposite. I do not like boys. I do not like them at all!"

"I brought you a line, but we will need to make a pole," Elsu said as he walked up behind her.

Angie turned to see Elsu's smile and immediately felt remorseful for jumping to conclusions. She jumped to her feet and was eager to catch her first fish.

After Elsu spent time showing Angie how to prepare a proper fishing pole and how to cast the line, Angie felt the frustration of casting out the line herself, over and over again. Elsu tried not to laugh at her awkwardness. His patience and her persistence helped Angie to become more adept at the skill. He praised her every time she made a good cast and she was finally able to get comfortable with the pole.

Waiting for the fish to bite was another challenge altogether. He had much more patience than she did, and she would get anxious for the fish to make its move. Suddenly, she felt a tug on her line.

"I think I caught a fish!" she yelled excitedly.

Elsu put his arms around Angie and showed her how to bring the fish in. At first, it bothered Angie to feel Elsu's arms around her, but the struggle of the fish took her mind off Elsu and on the struggle to win the fight. To show the boys that she could catch a fish too, to show Halona that she could help bring home food. The fish jerked back and forth, and the smile on her face was infectious. Elsu smiled as well and worked hard with Angie as they continued to drag the fish closer and closer to the shore.

"It is big!" Angie yelled.

Elsu laughed and kept up the tension until they both pulled the fish up on shore. Angie was so excited to see her large trout.

"It must be the biggest trout ever!" she boasted.

"One of the biggest," Elsu agreed.

She knelt down next to Elsu to watch him carefully gut and clean the fish. At first, the idea of cleaning the fish was appalling, but she was also fascinated to watch the process, since she intended to do it herself with the next fish she caught. When he was finished, he handed the fish to her. She looked down at the fish lying in her open palms and then looked up at Elsu and said, "Thank you!"

Elsu kept staring at Angie's eyes, and it was starting to make her uncomfortable. They were entirely too close, she realized. Suddenly, Elsu leaned over and kissed her gently on the lips. She was taken back by her first kiss, and alarm came over her. She jumped to her feet and said, "Do not ever do that again!"

She turned to leave, but stopped herself just long enough to throw the fish at him.

"You keep it!" she said as she quickly stomped up the hill to her camp. Elsu stared at her rash retreat, and then smiled to himself.

As she sat in front of the teepee that day, watching Halona weaving a basket, she couldn't help think about her first kiss. She didn't like it, but somehow, that kiss intrigued her. She decided she wouldn't tell anyone. All she knew was that she would keep her distance from Elsu from then on.

Angie was becoming bored with her daily chores and began looking for something to keep her interest, other than fishing. She felt too old for dolls and chasing crows from the corn fields, and she loved to watch the women of the village make baskets. She had asked Halona to teach her the craft, but Halona waved her away and said, "No time, no time."

A couple days soon after that, she was looking at the basket that Kimana's mother, Waneta, was weaving. She hesitated to ask, but soon heard the words coming out of her mouth, "Will you please teach me to weave a basket?"

"Yes, mother!" Kimana agreed, "Teach us!"

Before she knew it, Angie and Kimana were sitting next to Waneta and learning to weave their very first basket. Every spare minute Angie had, she sat with Kimana and Waneta working on weaving different colored reeds into a round form. It helped Angie forget about her crocheted blanket and discover a new outlet for her frustration.

When she finished her basket, she thought it looked wonderful, even though a bit crooked and uneven, and she was anxious to show it to Halona.

"Look Halona!" she said excitedly as she held up her basket proudly. "Look what I made!"

The old woman glanced at Angie's project, shook her head, and went back to weaving her own basket that showed many years of perfection.

Angie took her basket into the teepee and set it next to her bedding. Next to her Shoshone dress, it was her first personal belonging since coming to the village and she was very pleased with it.

This will be the first of many more, she told herself, *and I will make the most beautiful baskets in the village! Someday, Halona will be proud of me. Someday, I will see her smile.*

****

CHAPTER FOURTEEN

The Mountain War

The summer went quickly and Angie kept her distance from Elsu. Whenever he tried to talk to her, she immediately left, and soon he gave up trying to strike up any conversation with her. He still smiled when he saw her, and she still ignored him.

She continued to create baskets at a steady pace and it was evident that her craft was becoming perfected throughout the year. Since Halona didn't want them, she gave them away to different women of the village and they were grateful to have them.

Her 13th birthday came and went while they were at their winter camp, and the spring Sun Dance was another great cause for celebration. With this year's celebration, there also came much sadness as two hunters were killed during the buffalo hunt. Just before the celebration began, the business of the funerals needed to be taken care of. This was the first burial Angie had seen since her own family was laid to rest. But it was so different than what she had experienced before. The death ritual was not actually a burial, but more of a cremation. The bodies were wrapped in skins, and then their belongings, including their teepee and bedstead laid on top, for their "pilgrimage beyond". Then all was set on fire to be sent to the Great Spirit and a land beyond the setting sun.

Several days of mourning ensued and then the matter of the Sun Dance took place.

After returning to the mountains, the summer came soon and it was very hot early this year. Angie was with her friends gathering root bulbs for their evening meal when the dogs in the village began to bark frantically.

The girls all looked up from their work and saw two Shoshone scouts on horseback emerging through the forest at full speed, yelling warnings to the village across the river.

"Arapaho!" they yelled, "Arapaho are coming!"

Kimana, Chocheta and Leotie jumped to their feet.

"Run!" they yelled at Angie. "Run and hide!"

Angie looked frantic, "Why? Where do we go?"

"Come with me!" Kimana grabbed her hand and they ran to the forest behind the village.

As they crouched behind the trees some distance from the teepees, Angie asked, "What is happening?"

"The Arapaho, they want our land!" Kimana told her.

"We have plenty of food and water," Chocheta explained, "Their land is not so rich."

The men were mounting their horses, and the women were running into the forest all around them with the children and the old. Angie looked frantically for Halona and then saw her among the other widows.

Soon the horses were being driven into a fast gallop across the river and then they began disappearing through the trees. Angie saw Elsu riding his pony behind this father and the elders. Enyeto and Siwili rode out behind the warriors with all the other young men.

"They're too young!" Angie said horrified at the thought that they could be killed in battle.

"I worry for my brother," Leotie started to cry.

Amitola, Chocheta's mother, knelt behind the girls and put her hands on their shoulders. "Our men are very brave. We must ask the Great Spirit to protect them."

Amitola led Kimana, Chocheta and Leotie in chanting their prayer. Soon other voices all over the forest began to join in the chanting. Songs for strength and victory could be heard among the chanting.

Angie bowed her head, closed her eyes, and with hands clenched in prayer asked the God of her Fathers for his overwhelming grace and protection of this people.

Please God, she prayed, *spare these people. Bring the men of this village home safe. Please keep the Arapaho away and let there be peace again.*

War cries could be heard on the air. Clashes of spears on shields and some rifle shots brought fear to the women's hearts.

Have faith, Angie kept repeating to herself, *Have faith and believe God will take care of them, especially the young men. Please God,* she prayed, *be with them now!*

"If the Arapaho come through the trees toward our village," Amitola told the girls, "we must run. Keep your eyes alert and stay with me. I know a cave we can hide in."

The girls nodded in agreement and could hardly catch their breath as they watched each clearing in the trees. Their hearts were pumping wildly.

The fighting continued for a long time, and Angie thought she would faint for lack of strength as she kept forgetting to breathe.

Tears continued to stream down Leotie's face, her sobbing uncontrolled. Leotie's mother found her and hugged her close to her chest. "Siwili and your father will return to us. Do not fear," she comforted her daughter.

The sun was beginning to go down in the east, and the screams and war cries began to fade away with the light. Then the silence made the women just as fearful as the sounds of the fighting.

They held their places, waiting to see who would emerge from the trees, their husbands and sons, or the Arapaho. They were tired from watching, but they could not tear their eyes away, not now. They must be on guard to run.

The shadows were looming large against the grass and starting to protrude across the river. And then the sound of horse hooves.

"They are coming," Amitola whispered. The forest filled with women, children and the old, was completely silent. The horses were coming closer.

The women held their breath as the warriors appeared through the trees, and then cries of relief filled the cool of the early evening air. Shoshone warriors were returning, tired, bloody, and wounded, but it was the Shoshone that had won this day.

Angie uttered thanks to her God and jumped to her feet with the others, running to meet the men and young boys as they returned across the river. She searched for all those she knew, for friends and their fathers and brothers.

The women were holding and hugging their husbands, fathers and sons. People were grabbing the wounded off their mounts and taking them to their teepees, calling for the medicine man. At the back of the group came the warriors leading the horses with the fallen dead lying across the ponies' backs. Cries of dread and grief replaced the sound of cheers as women discovered who had sacrificed their lives for the good of the village.

Angie was relieved to see Siwili, and beside him rode Enyeto. Leotie and her mother ran to Siwili and his father as they returned, tired, but unscathed.

She looked for Elsu but didn't see him. With all the commotion, she didn't notice if he had returned with the living, wounded or dead.

Angie found Kimana and asked her if her father had returned alright. "Yes, he has a few wounds, but he is not hurt badly," Kimana told her and added, "Dyami, the man I will marry, is alright too."

"Have you seen Elsu?" Angie asked her.

"No, I only looked for my father and Dyami," she answered, "We will go to their teepee and see if Chief Nahele and his son have returned."

Angie suddenly felt a stream of dread flow through her body as they walked through the village toward Chief Nahele's tent. A lot of activity was surrounding his teepee and people were chanting.

"Why are they chanting?" Angie asked.

"Someone is wounded or someone is dead," Kimana told her.

They stood beyond the adults and waited to hear word of Chief Nahele and Elsu.

Then Chief Nahele emerged from his teepee. "My son, Elsu, fought the Arapaho and won. He shall live. His wounds are deep and he will need much rest."

Angie's heart leapt in her chest. She was not in love with Elsu, but he was her friend and she thanked God for bringing all those she knew home alive.

Twelve brave warriors died that day and the mourning continued for four days before all the dead were prepared for their pilgrimage and the funerals were completed.

As another week went by, news came that Elsu's wounds were healing. One arrow had found its mark in Elsu's side and another in his shoulder. He had lost a lot of blood, but no vital organs had been damaged.

Kimana and Leotie found Angie returning from the river with her washing that morning.

"We are going to take a gift to Elsu," Kimana said as she held some flatbread and Leotie had flowers in her hand. "Come with us."

"I will bring a gift too," Angie said and placed some berries and a couple prickly pears in one of her baskets. She was a little hesitant about going, but wanted to be a friend to Elsu.

When the girls arrived at Chief Nahele's teepee, he was sitting out in front with the elders, talking and smoking pipes with them. Elsu's mother, Eyota, was inside, tending to Elsu's wounds.

As they waited for Eyota to emerge from the teepee, Angie overheard the elders talking about the wagon train that had come through the land several days before.

A wagon train, Angie heard the words repeat themselves over and over again in her mind. Her heart leapt in her chest and she had the sudden urge to run and chase after the pioneers. The old familiar images of people of her own culture reminded her how much she missed her past. She tried hard to keep her feelings under control, knowing that the wagon train had already moved on and it would not be possible for her to find them.

Just then Eyota emerged from the teepee and gave permission to the girls to give Elsu his gifts. Elsu struggled to sit up when he saw the girls enter his tent. They each took turns setting their gifts down in front of him. Elsu's eyes stayed on Angie and he held the basket in his hands. She shied away and stood behind her friends.

"We had better go," Angie said.

"Stay," Elsu said, "I wish you to stay and talk."

The girls sat on the floor near his bedstead and Kimana did most of the talking. Angie responded only when asked a question, and Leotie only smiled, her shy side taking over.

Angie was uncomfortable because Elsu kept staring at her, and she wanted to leave. She suddenly, jumped to her feet and said, "Halona needs me. I must go now."

Angie found herself on the outside of the teepee before she could utter another word. She quickly began to walk away toward her camp.

"Wait!" Kimana called after her. "We are coming!" Kimana and Leotie came running up behind her.

"Why did you leave so fast?" Kimana asked her.

Angie shrugged her shoulders.

"I think Elsu likes you," Kimana continued.

Again Angie shrugged her shoulders. Kimana realized that Angie didn't want to talk about Elsu and thought Angie liked him too.

"Come with me," Kimana told her, taking her by the hand. "There is someone I want you to meet."

They walked to the other side of the village and stopped in front of a teepee. There Kimana called, "Dyami!"

A young woman came out of the teepee and glared at Kimana, saying, "He is not here. He is hunting."

She was obviously pregnant and looked ready to bear her child soon.

"I will come back another time," Kimana told her and the young woman turned and went back inside the teepee.

"Who was that?" Angie asked.

"That is his Dyami's first wife, Takhi," Kimana answered as they walked away.

"He is already married?" Angie was shocked.

"He married Takhi many years ago," Kimana told Angie. "They are finally blessed with a child."

"If he is married, how can you marry him?" Angie did not understand the Shoshone practice of several wives in a family.

"Many men die in hunting and in battle," Kimana tried to explain, "There are few men for many women. So that a woman will be cared for, many women marry one man."

"Do you like Takhi?" Angie asked her.

"She loves Dyami and does not want him to marry again," Kimana understood her situation.

"I am concerned for you," Angie told her.

"Why?!" Kimana reacted in surprise. "This is the way of the Shoshone. She will accept me the same as I would accept another wife if Dyami marries again after me."

Angie shook her head and knew that she could not accept this arrangement for herself. She would not share her husband if she were ever to marry. That was not the way of her culture and she became even more determined to be true to her own heritage.

"I do not understand why you fight against this belief," Kimana said to Angie, "it is the natural way of life. Look at the animals. The buck has his many deer in his herd. The buffalo fights for his females and has many. This is also the way of the Shoshone."

"You may believe what is best for you," Angie answered, "Just as I will believe what is best for me. I was raised with the teaching of one woman for one man, and they married because they were in love. That is what I want for my life."

Now it was Kimana's turn to shake her head, "I do not understand the silly teachings of the white man."

Angie took offense to Kimana's words, but decided it was best to keep the offense to herself. She didn't wish to argue the subject any longer and returned to her teepee to work on her basket.

How different are these people, Angie thought, *How different, and yet so much the same. The love of family, the kindness, the stubbornness, the fear, the bravery, and the teachings that each culture accepts as natural. Is this why people oppose each other? Is this what causes fighting and dissention? How sad. How sad are the differences. How sad are the conflicts they cause.*

****

CHAPTER FIFTEEN

The Baby

Elsu soon healed and was enjoying being outside with his friends again. He searched for Angie, but she avoided him whenever he came near her. He decided to wait until she was older before he would pursue her any further.

Angie was working on a new basket by her teepee when Kimana came running up to her.

"Angie, come!" Kimana yelled excitedly, "Takhi is having her baby!"

Halona, who was sitting nearby, just shook her head.

Angie jumped to her feet and ran behind Kimana until they reached the menstrual tent.

There were dozens of women and a few other girls waiting outside the tent. Dyami was not there. He was back at camp with the men waiting for the news of his first child.

Angie was taken aback by Takhi's screams of pain and it frightened her. She knew other women who had their babies while she had been at the village, but this was the closest to childbirth she had ever been. She looked at the other women's faces and they all seemed calm and some were even smiling. Women were quietly talking among themselves and others were chanting softly, almost like a song.

Almost an hour passed before Takhi's screams stopped and silence engulfed the entire area. A very weak cry could then be heard inside the tent. The cry of a newborn baby.

It was minutes more before Takhi's mother emerged from the tent and announced, "Dyami has a son!"

A roar of approval rose into the air. Kimana smiled broadly with the news. She looked proudly at Angie, almost like she had borne the child herself.

The word reached Dyami and he came walking quickly up to see this miracle of life. Angie recognized him from seeing him around the camp. Kimana had meant to introduce Angie to Dyami, but he had been away for days hunting with his friends. Now he had returned just in time for the birth of his baby.

Takhi's mother went back inside the tent and emerged again with a tiny baby wrapped in skins to keep him warm. She handed the baby to Dyami and he proudly held the boy up for all to see. The baby was so small, so very small. Tiny little cries came from under the wrapping.

The women all seemed to share his excitement and then began to disperse back to their camps.

"I have a new son!" Kimana celebrated as they walked back to the camp. "Did you see how handsome he is?"

"He is Takhi's son," Angie gently reminded her.

"He will be my son next spring when I marry Dyami," Kimana explained, "and I will love him as my own."

Angie understood what Kimana was trying to say, but the idea seemed unnatural to Angie, regardless.

The next morning the Medicine Man was summoned to Dyami and Takhi's teepee. Cries of anguish came from the tent and people began to gather once again. Dyami stormed from the teepee, mounted his horse, and rode off through the trees.

Angie found Kimana on her knees, rocking back and forth, tears streaming down her face, wailing along with her mother. Angie knelt down next to Kimana and said, "What has happened Kimana?"

Kimana cried, "He has died, he was too weak. Too small."

"I am sorry, Kimana," Angie said as she placed her hand on Kimana's shoulder.

"Go away," Kimana said to Angie through her sobs and then laid her head against her mother's chest.

Waneta looked sympathetically at Angie and then nodded that she should go.

Angie slowly raised to her feet and walked quietly away.

****

Angie was now well into her 14th year of age and found that she had a special way with her hands, crafting things the same as her mother had. She now made the most beautiful baskets in the village with new designs the women had never seen before. The Shoshone women would come by Halona's tent to see Angie's craftsmanship, but tried not to show their interest. They would feign the visit as just checking on Halona's welfare and to say a few words to the old widow. Kimana and Leotie began to learn the secrets of Angie's designs and also made replicas of the beautiful baskets which made the village women eager to hold and examine. No one would touch Angie's baskets as Halona made it very clear that the baskets Angie made belonged to Halona and no one else. Angie finally felt as though Halona had approved of her, or approved of her baskets anyway.

Chocheta was not interested in learning to make baskets. She was only interested in Enyeto and would wander down to the river to watch him fish, hoping he would notice her. She knew she was pretty and tried to use that fact to her advantage by flirting with him as often as she could. But Enyeto seemed to be more interested in his fishing than in Chocheta, much to her frustration.

As Angie grew, she also spent more time talking with God. She loved to go to the river by herself and tell Him her secret feelings and experience peace only He could give her. He knew her pain. He understood her frustrations. He answered her prayers.

Winter was well on its way as the village moved south and settled in the plains once more. Angie tried very hard to talk with Halona during the long walk, but Halona continued to ignore her.

Angie could not help but think about the wagon trains that continued to pass through the area several times a year, but she never knew when they were near. She could not stand to keep the subject to herself any longer.

"Halona," she said bravely, "I have heard there are wagon trains that pass through the land every summer. I want to go with them the next time they travel past our village."

"No!" Halona finally spoke, "You cannot go!"

"Why?" Angie tried hard to find the word as it stuck in her throat, fearing Halona's answer.

"You stupid girl!" Halona answered, "You must serve me. The elders have decided, you help me. I will not let you go. You stay with Shoshone people. No more talk!"

Angie knew Halona's mind was set.

After their camp was arranged, Angie walked down to the river to pray.

"God, help me. I cannot turn Halona's heart to accept me. What should I do?"

Angie thought about the Bible and what her mother had taught her about being 'kind to those who despitefully use you' and to 'love your neighbor as yourself'.

She knew God had heard her feeble prayer, but it would be hard to show love to an old bitter woman who despised her.

"I will try God," she said as she looked up into the heavens, "but you will have to help me. Please?"

Every day after that prayer, Angie tried very hard to be kind and respectful to Halona and smiled every time she saw the old woman, but it didn't seem to change Halona's attitude or demeanor. Every night, Angie prayed for strength to carry on 'loving' the old woman.

Love her. Just keep loving her. The words echoed over and over again in her mind.

The next morning was particularly beautiful. When Angie brought Halona her morning meal, she set the meal down before her, reached over and gave the old woman a gentle hug and kissed her on the cheek like she used to do with her mother.

Halona was so startled that she pushed Angie away and yelled at her "Do not do that again!" Halona snatched up her breakfast and began to eat.

Angie's heart was broken. An action that was an earnest effort had been rebuked and seemed so distasteful to the old woman. Angie felt foolish and wished she had never made the gesture.

"Why God? I've tried so hard." She had returned to the river and was talking to God. "I have tried so hard to love her, but she just rejects me like an old dog. How long can I keep up this pretense?"

And then the realization came to Angie that it was exactly that...a **pretense**.

"What is **real** love?" she asked God.

"Yes, love is patient, love is kind," Angie was struggling trying to remember the scripture she had heard from her father's knee. "And love is not a keeper of wrongs…"

She stopped herself. "Help me to love her, truly love her from deep within my heart." Angie prayed and felt a joy and peace enter her, as if she had just made a breakthrough. She smiled to herself and thanked God for her new revelation.

Angie began to see Halona with new eyes which brought warmth and caring for the old woman. The feeling flowed through her as she had never known before. And something strange began to happen to Halona. When Halona would raise her hand to strike Angie, she would suddenly stop herself and slowly lower her hand. Angie could see Halona deep in thought and struggling with her own feelings.

I don't know if Halona will ever like me, Angie thought to herself, *but perhaps she will grow to accept me. That would be enough.*

****

CHAPTER SIXTEEN

The Painted Bowl

That night Angie could not sleep because of the many images flooding her brain. Beautiful scenes of the village hand painted on pottery came drifting through her thoughts. Handsome young braves astride their horses and beautiful Indian maidens washing their clothing in the river. Peaceful fires lit near the teepees and older women grinding corn. The elders speaking wise words around the campfires and two hunters returning with their kill. Ospreys soaring above in the spring air looking for their next meal in the river below, and green trees full of fresh new leaves, and the soft grass of the valley. All were images Angie had come to know as home.

The very next morning Angie set out to collect clay from the riverside and began working it with her hands, molding and forming the shape she had seen in her mind. She added more water, smoothing the sides and working the clay until it began to hold together into a pleasing bowl of ample shape. But the bowl was too big and one side began to fall. She began again and again, each time being careful to add a little more dried reed grass until her bowl finally held its shape. She smoothed more clay around the sides and then set it out to dry in the hot sun.

She realized she had spent the entire day working on the bowl and began to panic when she realized she forgot to do her chores and prepare Halona's midday meal and now it was time for the evening meal. She hurried back to their teepee and quickly began preparing the food when Halona came out of the teepee and gave Angie a suspicious glare, but didn't utter a word, nor did she strike her. Angie was surprised that Halona had nothing to say and Angie vowed that she would not let that happen again.

The next morning, after preparing a meal for Halona, Angie hurried down to where she set her bowl out to dry.

Chocheta was picking the bowl up in her arms, preparing to take it back to the village.

"Look what I have found," Chocheta smiled.

"Put it down," Angie said as she approached, "It might not be dry yet."

"Is this bowl yours?" Chocheta asked as she carefully set it back down on the ground.

"Yes, I made it yesterday," Angie answered her, fearing her bowl may have cracked.

"What are you going to do with it?" Chocheta asked her.

After carefully examining the bowl, Angie answered, "I want to paint a picture on it, a very special scene of our village. I need to make some colors but I am not sure how to make the paint. I think I can use berries and…"

"I can help you. I have seen my father paint," Chocheta offered excitedly, "I will ask him what we need and we can collect it."

Chocheta ran to find her father, Maska, with Angie close behind her. When they reached Chocheta's teepee, the girls quizzed Maska about how to make paint. Maska laughed at his daughter's earnest plea and not being able to refuse her anything, he set about helping the girls collect just the right plants to make their colors.

Maska showed the girls how to find minerals in the earth, such as iron that makes a red color, and zinc that makes a white pigment. Ochre turns yellow and charcoal from the fire makes gray. He showed them which plants were best, like the Indigo plant that makes a medium blue color, leaves that are green, and berries that make a pink tint.

Even insects were gathered. Maska explained how the cochineal insect makes a deep red color and ground beetle shells can be used for black.

After gathering all the items they would need, Angie ran back to her teepee and prepared Halona's noon meal and then checked on her bowl. It was drying nicely and Angie was excited to begin her artwork.

When she returned to Chocheta's camp, Maska was grinding their collected items into powders.

Maska showed the girls how the minerals were ground into a powder, the insects boiled, dried and mashed into a powder, and the leaves were dried and ground into a powder of their own. Maska then gathered some eggs and used the yolks and some water to mix with the different powders. Maska explained to the girls that the egg yolks helped the powder to bind and stick to the surface they'd be painting on. To help the white powder to bind, Maska used some melted animal fat that he had saved from his other paintings. The yolk would turn his paint yellow, and he wanted a pure white color.

Angie was fascinated with all the different colors Maska was making and imagined where each color would be used on her bowl, picturing the scene in her mind.

Maska showed them his paintbrushes he had made by using carved wooden handles and horsehair tied with sinew to the handle. He then showed the girls how to properly make brush strokes in order to make the images appear, using a large rock as his canvas. Maska then smiled and gave each of the girls a paintbrush for them to start their creations with. Angie was very excited and thanked him repeatedly.

As Angie and Chocheta walked back to the river to check the dryness of her bowl, they noticed Enyeto examining her work of art. Elsu was with him.

"Please do not touch it!" Angie yelled so he could hear her as the girls approached.

"I will not break it," Enyeto rebuked her.

Angie knelt down and examined its texture, feeling the smoothness of the sides and gliding her fingers around the inside.

"It looks good," Enyeto told her. "Did you make it?"

"Yes," she answered, still examining the round piece of clay.

"I'm going to make one too," Chocheta added as she coyly smiled at Enyeto. Her growing affection for him showed on her face.

Seeing the brush in Angie's hand, Enyeto asked, "What are you going to paint?"

"This bowl," she answered him, "I want to paint a picture of our village on it."

"Where is your paint?" Elsu asked her and then added, "I will teach you to make it."

"Chocheta's father has already taught me," Angie told him and then picked up the bowl and carried it to Chocheta's teepee. There, Angie began to paint her images on the sides of the clay bowl.

Angie had seen very little of Kimana in the past month. Kimana wished to spend her free time with Dyami, which added to Takhi's pain. Takhi felt she had lost her son, and now she was in danger of losing her husband. Kimana would marry Dyami this spring during the Sun Dance ceremony and Takhi feared the competition for Dyami's attention. She waited many years to learn that she was with child, and was afraid she might have to wait many more years to offer Dyami another baby. She didn't understand why the Sun god did not hear her prayers for many children. She knew a child would be a huge source of pride for

Dyami and she wanted to please him. Her feelings of failure were beginning to drive her into a deep depression.

Without Kimana coming to see Angie, Leotie seemed to stay to herself and rarely left her family's camp.

Each day, Angie went to Chocheta's tent where she spent her free time working on the bowl, and each day, Chocheta's family gave her their approval of her progress. Maska was patient, teaching Angie the secrets of his art, and she absorbed his words like a sponge. Chocheta never did make a bowl of her own, but she loved to watch Angie paint and encouraged her creativity.

Several weeks later, Angie's bowl was finished. She set it down to dry and admired how it turned out. The women who lived nearby came to view the beautiful painting and Amitola was proud to show them, as if Angie were her own daughter.

That afternoon Angie came into the teepee and nervously set her completed work of art down in front of Halona. The old woman looked up at Angie in bewilderment and after just a few moments, Halona got to her feet and left the tent.

Angie sat down, trying hard not to cry. She had tried so hard to please Halona. She wanted to give her something from her heart.

No matter what I do, she thought to herself, *I cannot please her. God, why is she so difficult? All I want to do is make her happy. I love her with all my heart, just the way I should. Will she ever be able to love me in return? Will I ever be able to please her? Ever?*

It was at that moment that Halona appeared through the opening of the teepee. In her arms she held the massive balls of yarn. Halona laid them down in front of Angie and then promptly left the tent again.

Angie's mouth fell open and her eyes widened as she slowly reached over and touched her yarn. A smile spread over her face. Her heart flooded with elation and waves of emotion flowed through her.

"My yarn," she told herself, "My yarn!"

Tears of happiness began to flow as she held each ball of yarn.

"Thank you, God!" she said as she looked up imagining Him towering over her in the teepee. "Thank you so much!"

****

CHAPTER SEVENTEEN

The Marriage Day

Maska helped Angie carve a crochet needle from oak wood, just as Angie had described it to him.

"This tool will be strong," Maska said as he sanded it to make it smooth.

He smiled as he handed it to Angie. Chocheta and her sister, Sisika, were admiring the different colors of yarn, handling each one. Angie showed the girls how to chain a long row and then began to crochet her design with the yarn, being careful to stitch in blessings just as her mother had taught her. Chocheta and Sisika laughed at Angie each time she added a blessing, but were soon dreaming up some of their own for Angie to stitch into the blanket.

In the mornings, Angie took her blanket to Chocheta's family's camp as they wanted to watch her work. Even Amitola added blessings to the blanket. The women from around the village came to sit with Amitola and watch Angie stitch the 'blessing' blanket, fascinated by the colored string.

In the afternoon, Angie would work on her blanket at her own camp. Halona was not interested in the blanket. She would just shake her head as Angie named each blessing being stitched.

"Silly girl," Halona told her. "You are silliest girl Halona knows."

"Where did you hide my yarn?" Angie asked Halona one day.

Halona didn't respond, but Angie kept asking.

"I give it to Haiwee, "Halona told her, "She keep it for me."

Haiwee was an old widow who lived on the other side of the village. She was a kind old woman and one who spent her time with the other widows. Not once did Haiwee let on that she had the yarn. She kept her promise to Halona.

As the blanket began to take shape, winter was beginning to fade. The cold was easing and there were new buds on the trees. Angie realized she must have turned 15 years old by now. One day ran into another here. Only the seasons mattered.

Angie missed her relationship with her old friends. It was good to spend time with Chocheta and her family, but it was not the same. She especially missed Kimana. She set her blanket down and walked to Kimana's camp. Kimana saw her coming and came to meet her. The girls hugged each other and Kimana began to cry.

"I miss you," Angie told her.

"I too miss you," Kimana told her, "I am sorry for how I behaved."

"What do you mean?" Angie asked her.

"When Dyami's baby died, I was very angry," Kimana said, "at everyone. I did not want to talk about our pain. It was easier not to see you. Not to see Chocheta or Leotie. Only Dyami. We mourned together."

"Is Takhi alright?" Angie asked her.

"She is very sad," Kimana told Angie, "she does not talk."

Angie nodded as she understood the deep feelings that loss brings.

"I will marry soon," Kimana said. "Will you come to the ceremony?"

"Of course," Angie smiled, "I will be there."

The girls hugged again and then a feeling of closeness came over them.

"Come," Angie said as she took Kimana by the hand. "Let us go find Chocheta and Leotie and talk. We need to talk. Tell us all about Dyami and your wedding."

The girls sat by the river and talked for hours, laughing and enjoying the renewal of their friendship. Laughter was replaced by tears and hugs, and then the laughter returned. It felt so good to Angie to feel a part of this circle of friends again.

As Angie returned to her tent, Kimana walked with her. Angie wanted to show her the bowl she'd made and the blanket she was working on. Soon after Halona received her gift from Angie, she set the bowl out in front of the teepee to proudly display it. Kimana was surprised how beautiful the painting was and she was amazed by the crocheted blanket.

"I have not seen anything like this," Kimana held the blanket in her hands, examining the design. "It is very beautiful. Will you give it to me...as a wedding gift?"

Angie began to stutter, "I cannot. It is all I have left of my family."

Kimana nodded sadly and then walked away, back to her camp.

Angie would do almost anything for Kimana and she felt guilty for not giving the blanket to her. The more she considered the idea, the more her heart ached.

"I cannot," she told herself. "I just cannot part with it."

****

The Sun Dance ceremony was only days away. Kimana spent more time preparing to be married than being with her friends. When she did come to see Angie, she always asked to see the blanket. Angie had finished the blanket some weeks before and it looked just as beautiful as it did when she made it many years ago. The old feeling of comfort had returned whenever she wrapped it around herself. The image of her mother came flooding back to her and she smiled whenever she thought about her family.

Angie was praying by the river, spending some alone time with God. In the middle of her prayer a voice spoke to her. It was Elsu, sitting down beside her.

"I have come to talk with you," he said.

"What do you wish to talk to me about?" Angie asked him.

"I am almost grown," Elsu explained. "It is time for me to take a wife. I have chosen you."

Angie knew this day might come and she started to panic.

"I am too young to marry," Angie explained.

"You are getting old," Elsu laughed. "Many girls marry years earlier."

"I am not ready to marry anyone," she insisted.

Elsu remained patient. "Next year, at the Sun Dance, we will marry."

Angie was frustrated and didn't know how to reason with Elsu. His culture was so different from her own.

"You do not understand," she began.

"Enough talk!" Elsu held up his hand, "It is settled." He got to his feet and walked back into the village.

She watched him walk away, stunned, and then looked up at the sky.

Oh God, she prayed, *I am afraid. I don't want to marry Elsu! You are the only one who can help me. I have tried to be faithful to you. I have tried to be good. Please help me! Please!*

She then lowered her head and felt a deep depression come over her.

****

The evening of the marriages had arrived. Many girls were preparing to become new wives, including Sisika, Chocheta's sister.

"It will be our turn soon," Chocheta said excitedly as she stood next to Angie waiting for the ceremony to begin.

Angie didn't react to Chocheta's excitement. Elsu's words kept running through her mind and it upset her.

"You will marry Elsu next year, and I will marry Enyeto," Chocheta smiled, "we will always be good friends, almost sisters."

"Who told you I will marry Elsu?" Angie started to panic again.

"Elsu told Siwili. Siwili told Leotie," Chocheta answered, "and Leotie told me you are promised."

"No, I am not promised," Angie assured Chocheta, "I have not agreed to marry Elsu."

"If Elsu wants to marry you," Chocheta said, "you will marry Elsu."

Angie wanted to change the subject and asked, "When did Enyeto ask you to marry him?"

"He has not asked yet," Chocheta confided, "but I know he will ask me soon."

"I am happy for you," Angie said and gave her friend a hug.

"And I am happy for you," Chocheta smiled.

Angie wished she could share her happiness, but the feelings just weren't there.

A group of men sitting around large drums started to play and sing in unison, along with men playing flutes that serenaded the spiritual leader as he led Dyami and Kimana to the center of the gathered crowd. The Holy Man performed a ceremonial washing of hands to wash away past evils and memories of past loves. Then the traditional poem was read;

O Morning Star! When you look down upon us, give us peace and refreshing sleep.

Great Spirit! Bless our children, friends, and visitors through a happy life.

May our trails lie straight and level before us. Let us live to be old.

We are all your children and ask these things with good hearts.

Dyami and Kimana then exchanged a piece of jewelry which was considered a shield against poverty and all types of evil.

The spiritual leader pulled hair from both Dyami and Kimana's head and tied it together. The bound hair represented that they were bound together, to be true to their mate at all times, chaste in thought, and to always remember their marriage vows.

More songs were sung as the new couple departed the circle as husband and wife.

Angie thought Kimana looked beautiful in her white skinned dress decorated with all kinds of colorful beading and a band of beads placed gracefully on her head. Dyami looked proud of his new wife, and Kimana was excited to be the center of attention. Takhi's absence was painfully obvious and Angie felt bad for her.

There were more marriages to follow, including Sisika's vows with her new husband. And then the celebrations began, feasting and music and dancing which lasted all night. People were laughing and songs filled the air.

Angie was enjoying watching the dancing when Elsu walked up next to her.

"We shall soon be husband and wife as they are," he said to Angie.

Angie turned to him and said, "Why do you want to marry me?"

"I am the son of a chief," Elsu answered, "You are a chieftain's daughter. It is a good match."

"I am not a chieftain's daughter," Angie said ashamed of her deception. "I said that to impress my friends."

"You let the tribe believe a lie?" Elsu grew angry. "A true Shoshone does not lie. I think all white men tell lies, and white women too!"

With that, Elsu stormed away. Angie felt a mixture of guilt and relief.

It's over, Angie smiled to herself. *Elsu will no longer want me. I'm free!*

The rest of the night, Angie relaxed and enjoyed the festivities. She felt as if a weight had been lifted from her shoulders. She felt lighter than air and wanted to yell out in joy.

Angie handed Kimana and Dyami her wedding gift, a beautiful basket she had made for Kimana. She noticed that Kimana glanced at the basket, looked disappointed, and set the basket aside. Angie knew Kimana was hoping for the colorful crocheted blanket, but Angie gave Kimana the best she could. Her blanket was out of the question.

As she laid herself down to sleep that night, her blanket brought her the usual comfort that Angie craved; the closeness of her mother, the closeness of her family from her past. The tighter she wrapped the blanket around her, the better she felt.

Thank you Lord, that I am free of Elsu. He is a good person, but I am not in love with him. Please bless Kimana and Dyami and help them to be good to each other. Give them many babies if that is what they want. Give them many days of happiness and may Kimana make wise choices.

****

CHAPTER EIGHTEEN

The Rescue

The mountain people returned to their summer home soon after the Sun Dance celebration, and several weeks had passed before Chocheta, Angie and Leotie saw Kimana again.

"How is it to be married?" Chocheta excitedly asked Kimana.

Kimana looked at her and answered, "It is alright."

"Tell me," Chocheta insisted, "how does it feel to have a man in your arms?"

Kimana didn't answer her.

Angie, feeling Kimana's sadness, said, "I think we should ask her later, when she has had more time as a wife."

Chocheta was disappointed, but didn't press Kimana any further.

Angie didn't see much of Kimana after that. Kimana was busy with her own camp and providing meals for her husband. Dyami was a possessive man and kept her friends away.

That afternoon, Angie went down to the river to pray and to spend her daily time with God. As she closed her eyes and whispered her words to God, she heard a voice next to her.

"What are you doing?" Enyeto asked as he sat down next to her.

"Praying," Angie answered.

"To which god?" he asked her.

"There is only one God I pray to," Angie answered him.

"You have only one god?" he laughed, "We have many gods who help the Shoshone people."

"I need only one God," Angie told him. "He is powerful and can do everything."

"Can he turn your hair black?" Enyeto teased.

"If he wanted to," Angie answered, "but why would He want to do that?"

"So you will look like Shoshone," Enyeto reasoned.

"I like my hair just the color He made it. I like the way I was created," she explained. "And I like you just the way you were made, and Kimana just the way she is made, and Leotie just the way she is made and Chocheta just the same. Everyone is made to be just as they are."

Enyeto stared at her. "You like me just the way I am?"

"Of course," she smiled, "God made you special, just like He made me special."

"And everyone is special," Enyeto laughed suspiciously, "If that is so, do you like Halona just the way she is? Is she special?"

"Yes, she is special," Angie answered thoughtfully, "She has a lot of pain she is trying to hide. But she is special in her own way."

Enyeto shook his head and got to his feet. "I do not understand you, Angie Owens. You are truly different from anyone I have known before. I will think on what you say, but your words are confusing to me."

Then Angie watched Enyeto walk on down the path to the village.

Angie smiled to herself. She was happy she got to share her God with Enyeto. This was the first time someone in the village wanted to know about the God she believed in. She rose to her feet and walked back to her tent, thinking about the words she shared with Enyeto. As she started to enter her teepee she was surprised to see Halona gently stroking Angie's crocheted blanket. A faint smile was on Halona's face and she was singing quietly to herself.

Angie stepped back, exiting the teepee, without Halona seeing her there. She was puzzled by Halona's behavior and all kinds of thoughts entered her head.

Does she really like my blanket after all? Angie asked herself, *Has she been trying to cover her true feelings all this time? I'm just not sure.*

As she walked away from the teepee, Elsu caught her by arm. She was surprised to see him smiling at her.

"I have decided we will still marry," he told Angie, "This lie will stay between us. No one else must know."

"I do not understand why you insist on marrying me," Angie tried to get Elsu to listen to her. "You are my friend, but I'm not ready to marry anyone. I am not in love with you, Elsu."

"After we are married," he said gently, "you will learn to respect me. Then you will learn to love me. It is the way of nature. It is the way of the Shoshone."

****

Enyeto returned to the river the next day when he saw Angie praying.

"I want to ask more questions about this God of yours who can do all things," he said as he sat down beside her.

"I do not know if I can tell you everything you want to know," she told him, "but I will tell you what I know about Him. I had a book once that told all about Him, but I lost it in the river. I wish I had it now."

They spent the next several hours discussing spiritual matters, and Angie was surprised how easily the answers came to her. The words of scripture from her father and mother came flooding back into her memory.

"We shall discuss this further," Enyeto said as he rose to his feet, "I want to know more."

As Enyeto walked away, she was surprised to see Kimana coming to the river with her washing.

"Kimana," Angie smiled. "It has been a long time since we talked."

"Yes it has," Kimana agreed, and the two girls hugged each other.

"Are you alright?" Angie asked, concerned for Kimana's welfare.

She nodded her head and then confided, "I wish I had not married Dyami."

"What has happened?" Angie asked, and looked intently into Kimana's eyes.

"He is mean to me," Kimana answered, "He hits me if I try to talk about things that bother me. Takhi is also mean to me. I think she has a jealous nature and does not like me."

"Maybe we should talk to Chief Nahele about this," Angie suggested.

"No," Kimana shook her head, "that would not be wise. A woman does not complain about her husband. It would be disrespectful and I will bring shame to my camp."

"How can I help you?" Angie asked her.

"You cannot help," Kimana smiled at her friend, "Do not marry, Angie. Only marry for love, as you told me. You are much wiser than me."

"Kimana," Angie said, touching her friends arm. "you can come stay with me. You do not need to be with them."

"Thank you, my friend," Kimana said, "but I will stay where I belong. I will soon have a family with Dyami and my children will need their father."

"Oh no," Angie warned her. "Do not have any children with him. If he is mean to you, he might be mean to your children also."

"It is too late," Kimana looked sad, "I am with child now."

"Oh Kimana," Angie tried to keep from crying and put her arms around her friend.

"Dyami will not hurt the child." Kimana explained, "To have a child is his heart's desire. A child will bring him pride, more than a wife will. To give him a child may be the only way I can obtain his approval, as long as Takhi poisons his mind against me."

"I'm sorry she has not accepted you," Angie told Kimana.

"Now that I am pregnant, she is bitter and feels that I am her enemy," Kimana confided, "Angie, I am not her enemy. I want to be her family, but she will not allow that to happen."

"I will pray for you." Angie said gently, "I will pray for you and your child."

Kimana nodded her head, "Yes, I am thankful for your prayers."

Angie helped Kimana wash her clothes and the girls talked about earlier days. They laughed and rejoiced in being together again.

"Kimana, come!" Dyami was standing behind them. "You have been away too long."

Kimana got immediately to her feet and grabbed her wet clothes.

Angie smiled to Dyami and greeted him, but he only motioned for Kimana to leave with him. As they walked back to their camp, Kimana turned and smiled at Angie. She returned her smile and waved to Kimana. She wondered if it would be a long time before she saw her again.

****

Angie spent the next few weeks allowing Elsu to talk about their future, without adding to his dreams. He knew she wasn't listening to his words, but he continued to talk, hoping he might say something that would catch her interest and persuade her. She felt numb inside when it came to her feelings for Elsu. She didn't love him, or hate him. She felt nothing at all.

But Angie's favorite moments were spent alone by the river, talking to God. As she was in the midst of her prayer one day, she suddenly had an impulse to open her eyes. Just at that moment she spotted Kimana's little brother falling headfirst into the river. She jumped to her feet and ran to where she saw him fall in. He was coming back up, and then he sank down, his little body being dragged down the river. She jumped into the water and swam as quickly as she could toward the floundering child. He came up one more time, struggling for air, and then he started to sink like a stone.

Just as he was almost out of reach, Angie was able to grab his arm and pull him to the surface. The little boy coughed up water and was grasping to reach something to hold on to. By now, she had her arm firmly around the boy and was swimming back to shore using the other arm.

Kimana's mother had just reached the shoreline, realizing that her son was missing. Her face was terrified as she saw Angie with her little boy, struggling to get back to shore. She was yelling for help, bringing villagers running to the river. Several men jumped in the water and pulled them safely to shore where Angie gasped for air. The little boy was crying in his mother's arms, and she was sobbing tears of relief. Kimana and her mother hugged Angie, thanking her over and over again for rescuing their precious son and brother.

"I thank your God for bringing you to us," Kimana held Angie in her arms. "If you had not been here, my brother would be dead."

The rest of the day, Angie thought about the near tragedy and how God enabled her to be there to save a little boy's life. She also thought about Enyeto's new interest in her God, and that made her smile.

Maybe, I am meant to be here, she thought to herself, *Maybe this has been God's plan for me all along. Maybe God has a reason for me living among the Shoshone that I did not see before. Dear God, if you wish me to stay among these people and not return to my own, then I am willing to do as you want me to. It is not my first desire, but if I have a purpose here, I am willing to stay.*

****

CHAPTER NINETEEN

The Return

It was the middle of summer and the days were hot and the sun baked down on the women's backs as they dug roots and planted more corn in the fields. After her chores were completed, Angie walked back to her favorite spot by the river to pray. Enyeto was waiting for her.

"Come sit down," he said as he patted the ground. "I have more questions for you."

She smiled and sat down beside him, looking forward to sharing with him.

"You say that you have one god, but then you talk about three," he began, "How can one god be three gods?"

As Angie tried to explain the Holy Trinity to Enyeto, she was unaware that Chocheta was watching them from behind the trees. Chocheta couldn't hear their words very well, but she noticed that they were very intent on talking with each other, and jealousy began to rise in her heart. The more she watched them talk and laugh, the more her anger grew.

Chocheta had convinced herself that Enyeto liked Angie more than he should. And she felt that Angie liked him in return. Her life with Enyeto felt threatened, and she turned and ran back to her camp. Once she arrived, she paced back and forth working herself up into a frenzy. Her imagination was running wild. Evil thoughts and evil plans were taking place in her mind. She wouldn't let Angie have Enyeto. He was hers. She had to stop them from seeing each other. Without thinking it through, she ran to Elsu and called him out of his teepee.

"What is it?" Elsu asked Chocheta.

"I have to tell you something I saw," Chocheta was breathing hard, her eyes wide, "I saw Angie with Enyeto, and they were kissing."

Elsu was silent for a few moments. He clenched his jaw and said, "Are you sure of what you saw?"

"Yes, I am sure," she lied to Elsu, "I watched them for a long time."

"Where are they?" Elsu demanded.

"By the river," Chocheta pointed north of the village.

Elsu was furious. He stomped his way to the river, fists clenched, with Chocheta close behind him. As he approached the river, he could hear Enyeto and Angie laughing. Seeing them sitting beside each other, his rage became uncontrollable and he grabbed Enyeto and Angie by the hair, pulling them to their feet.

"Liars, cheaters!" he screamed in their faces. "I trusted you both!"

"What are you saying?" Enyeto yelled, pulling his hair out of Elsu's clutches. Elsu let go of Angie's hair and shoved her to the ground.

"You know she is to be my wife!" Elsu yelled at Enyeto, pointing to Angie. "But you have betrayed me as a friend."

Then he turned to Angie. "You are unfaithful. You have an evil spirit in you. You will be punished for your misdeeds!"

Both Enyeto and Angie were stunned.

"What have we done?" Enyeto insisted.

"You have been seen kissing each other!" Elsu accused, "What else have you done?!"

"We have done none of this," Enyeto defended himself and Angie.

"Liar!" Elsu yelled and hit Enyeto in the face with his fist, causing him to reel back on his heels.

"No!" Chocheta yelled at Elsu, "Do not hit him!"

Elsu's anger was too far gone and he continued to hit Enyeto until he fell to the ground. Angie scrambled to her feet and ran to get help.

Chocheta stood by, hands clasped to her mouth, her eyes wide with fear for Enyeto.

Enyeto got to his feet and began to defend himself, striking Elsu with all his strength.

"Help!" Angie screamed as she ran to Elsu's tent, "Help! Elsu and Enyeto are fighting!"

"Where?" Chief Nahele asked, getting quickly to his feet.

Chief Nahele and several of the elders ran to the river where they saw the two young men, bloody and wrestling on the ground, punching each other with clenched fists.

As the men tried to pull Elsu and Enyeto apart, Chocheta grabbed Angie's hand. "Come, you are in big trouble."

The two girls ran to Chocheta's camp.

"Here," Chocheta said, handing Angie the reins to her father's horse. "Go. Ride away from here. You must leave while you can. Elsu will surely want revenge on you."

Frightened to the core, Angie mounted the horse and began to ride through the trees, down the river that was out of sight from the village, and crossed it at the shallow end at full speed. Water splashed up all around her, but her eyes were set on the forest ahead of her. She managed to guide the horse through the trees and out into the open prairie.

It wasn't until she felt safe that she brought the horse to a stop. Her heart was still pounding and her body shaking with fear. She tried to control herself and get a grasp of where she was. Suddenly a different kind of fear took over her. The fear of being on her own, lost in the wilderness, not knowing which direction to go.

"Where do I go from here?" she asked God, "What should I do?"

It was then that she saw dust rising in the distance. The dust of many animals.

"The Shoshone!" she gasped, "They are coming for me! Elsu is probably with them!"

She went to turn the horse to run when she heard the familiar sound of wagon wheels, a sound she hadn't heard for a very long time. She stopped herself, and strained to hear if she heard the sound correctly. Her eyes searched the dust to see if her imagination was playing tricks on her.

They were not. A wagon train was making its way west, heading in her direction. She turned the horse toward the flying dust and galloped to make up the distance, slowing down as she got closer.

Thank you God! she smiled. *Thank you for your perfect timing. You truly are amazing! I'm going home!*

Rifles were raised and wagons stopped as the pioneers saw her approaching on the Indian horse in her Indian garb. Her blonde hair was blowing in the wind, making a contradictory impression on the people who stood before her. Confused, the emigrants stood their ground and didn't lower their rifles until she came close to the wagon train. The wagon master rode out to meet her and saw her large smile as she yelled, "I am Angie Owens from Columbia, Missouri!"

She was struggling to say the words. Finding English was no longer her first language. The wagon master and Angie came to a stop and he looked at her dark tanned skin and bright blue eyes.

"Where have you been, young lady?" he asked her.

"I have been living with the Shoshone," she told him, "I want to go back to my people. Are you traveling to California?"

He smiled and said, "Yes, would you like to join us?"

Her face beamed. "Yes please, that would be wonderful!"

They rode back to the wagon train together.

Rifles were lowered, and again, Angie was the object of stares.

"This little lady has been living with the Indians and wants to go home to California. Is there a family willing to take her with them?" The wagon master asked.

After a few empty minutes, a voice spoke up, "She can ride with us. We have room for her!"

Angie felt relief flow over her and smiled at the man who raised his hand.

"Well, it's settled then," the wagon master said. "You can go with them." He turned toward the rest of the wagon train and shouted, "Circle up. We'll spend the night here."

She rode the horse over to the family who welcomed her with large smiles.

"My word!" the woman said as Angie approached her, "I never thought I'd see the likes of you out here in the wilds."

Angie climbed down from the horse. "My name is Angie Owens, from Columbia Missouri." She was still struggling with her English, but the words were starting to come back to her.

"I'm Mary Turner, this here is my husband, Joshua, and our two sons, Mathew and Mark," she introduced her family, "Are you heading for California?"

"Yes," Angie nodded. "I'm going to live with my aunt and uncle in Sacramento. My parents died many years ago." The reality of being back with the wagon train heading west was starting to overwhelm her.

Angie spent the night sitting around the campfire and talking about her experience living with the Shoshone tribe. The Turners were fascinated and could not believe it when daybreak was already appearing in the sky.

The morning bugle signaled it was time to rise and prepare to move on.

"I must go back to the village," Angie jumped to her feet. "I have left something there that's very important. And I need to return Maska's horse. He has been very good to me and I will not steal from him."

"You can't go back," Mary warned, "they might not let you go with us."

"Or worse," Mathew agreed, "They could hurt you."

Angie thought about their words. "The Shoshone are good people. They won't hurt me. I'll return the horse, gather my belongings and return. Please wait for me."

"We'll wait," Joshua agreed, "but how will you get back?"

"I'll take Halona's mule, if she will allow it," Angie suggested, "or I'll run, but I will return as soon as I can."

"I'll go with you," Mathew said as he stood up, "You can ride with me on my horse."

He picked up his rifle and added, "I'll make sure you return."

"You won't need that," Angie said, looking at the weapon.

"I'll bring it just in case," Mathew remarked as he went to saddle up one of their horses.

"I'm coming too," Mark said as he jumped to his feet. Mark was younger than Mathew, about 16 years old, and anxious to help Angie.

"You're staying right here," Mary instructed her son. "One son in danger is enough. Don't need both of you going into who knows what."

Angie mounted Maska's horse, while Mathew gave his mother a kiss on her cheek.

"We'll be back soon. Then we can catch up with the wagon train," Mathew smiled.

"Take care of yourself, son," Mary smiled, with fear in her eyes.

"God go with you," Joshua said as he put his hand on Mathew's shoulder.

With that, Mathew climbed up on his horse and rode toward the forest beside Angie.

****

The word spread fast that Angie had returned to the village with a white man. Chief Nahele, the elders and many others left their camps and went to Halona's teepee to see what was happening.

Angie's friends followed close behind and pushed their way through the other onlookers to see Angie.

Mathew sat nervously on his horse, but didn't move or say a word.

Angie soon emerged from their teepee carrying her crocheted blanket of many colors. "I am leaving," she told all those that stared at her. "I am going back to my people. I am going far away to the west to live with my relatives. The wagon train will take me."

"No, you cannot go!" Kimana cried as she ran to Angie and held her tight.

"I must go, Kimana," Angie said gently, "It is where I belong."

Chocheta approached Angie. "I told the truth, Angie. I told Elsu and Enyeto that I lied. I did not see you and Enyeto kissing. I am sorry for the trouble I caused you. Please forgive me."

Angie smiled at Chocheta as tears began to run down the beautiful Indian girl's face. She hugged Chocheta and said, "I forgive you. I love you."

Elsu stood silently in front of the crowd, bruised and cut in more ways than one. His feelings were mixed. Would he object to letting her go? He felt the panic of separation in his heart but his head was struggling with what was right and what was wrong.

Chief Nahele looked at his son. "She needs to go to her people. It is best for her. She will be content there."

Others muttered their agreement, while her friends grieved. Angie walked up to Leotie who had silent tears running down her cheeks. "I will miss you," Angie said. "Be of good cheer. You are so special."

Then she turned back to Kimana, "You are my special friend, and I will love you always." Kimana was greatly grieved.

"Maybe we will see each other again," Kimana hoped.

Angie nodded and then kissed her gently on the cheek. She turned to see Halona sitting alone by their teepee, staring at the ground and stirring the dirt with a stick. Angie approached Halona with a smile on her face and knelt beside her. "May it always keep you warm." Angie laid the blanket of blessings in Halona's lap. She then hugged Halona warmly, kissed her on the cheek and whispered in her ear, "I love you, Halona."

The old woman looked up at Angie, tears forming in her eyes. Halona ran her feeble fingers over the crocheted yarn and whispered, "This stitch is for love, and this stitch is for kindness...," her voice trailing away.

Angie swung on behind Mathew onto his horse, to return to the wagon train.

Enyeto ran to stop Angie. "Angie Owens, I am glad you came to the Shoshone. I did not like you when you came to our village, but you have brought good to our people. I will miss you."

"I will miss you too, Enyeto," she smiled.

"You may call me Pearl Stinkbody. Tell the white man about me."

"I will tell them about **Enyeto**," Angie looked at him with tenderness, "it is a much better name for you."

She turned to the crowd and said, "May God be good to you as you have been good to me."

"Goodbye, my daughter," Halona whispered.

She smiled and waved goodbye to the village who had gathered. Her eyes began to tear for the first time since she came to this village. She was leaving the people who were her family and whom she came to love.

As they rode back through the forest, Angie realized she was returning to her own people who pioneered the trail west. She was looking forward to finishing her trek to Sacramento and the life she would find there.

****

Would you like to see your manuscript become a book?

If you are interested in becoming a PublishAmerica author, please submit your manuscript for possible publication to us at:

acquisitions@publishamerica.com

You may also mail in your manuscript to:

**PublishAmerica
PO Box 151
Frederick, MD 21705**

www.publishamerica.com

CPSIA information can be obtained at www.ICGtesting.com
Printed in the USA
BVOW061711090312

284852BV00001B/31/P

9 781462 653508